Tossed

A Snack-Sized Mystery Cruise

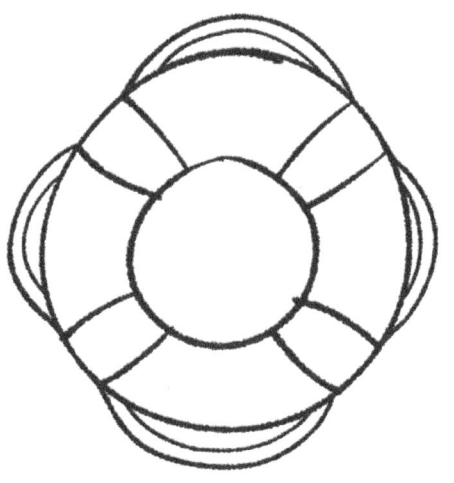

TOSSED

A Snack-Sized Mystery Cruise

Jeff Schmoyer

Jmars Ink

Copyright © 2023 Jeff Schmoyer

All rights reserved. No portion of this book may be reproduced in any form without written permission from the author, except as permitted by U.S. copyright law.

This is a work of fiction. Unless otherwise indicated, all the names, characters, businesses, places, events and incidents in this book are either the product of the author's imagination or used in a fictitious manner. Any resemblance to actual persons, living or dead, or actual events is purely coincidental.

Art by Ani Sledgianowski
Back cover waves by Lionello Delpiccolo, Unsplash

Published by Jmars Ink
Visit JmarsInk.com

ISBN 979-8-9881866-2-5

Acknowledgments

A feast of thanks to my fabulous beta readers
Deborah L Brewer and Robert Spiller.

Chapter One

"Man overboard!"

It was like in the movies—the shrieking alarm and the repeated, "Man overboard!" blaring over loudspeakers. But this was all too real. Crew members rushed past me in the darkness towards the back of the ship. Passengers ran behind with morbid curiosity, or they could be running to help though I didn't see how untrained members of the public would be of any use.

The behemoth that had been my lodging for the last four days lurched and I was shoved along the slippery deck and against a railing by the stampeding herd as the ship tried to turn and stop so as not to leave a drowning person in its wake in the middle of the Atlantic. This was not what I had signed up for.

But as a denizen of the Internet, pre-embarking research had told me that someone died onboard a commercial cruise all too often. Of course, people died all the time and they had to do it somewhere, but why did so many of them have to do it around me?

I was not usually this whiney, but my stomach was roiling and I was afraid I could be next. I hastened back to my cabin at my tummy's behest and to make sure my mother was safe.

Chapter Two

Four days earlier I had been filled with great expectations. I had never been on an ocean cruise before and the thought of it was both exciting and daunting.

As my mother and I waited to board in the slow-moving security queue, I surveyed the Queen Alex 2 docked in New York Harbor. The skyscraper-sized ship, trimmed in red over a black and white steel hull, looked as if it had been created for another time. A time that was more elegant—one filled with a classier class of people than me.

I walked the gangplank with my mother on my arm and we entered the multi-story lobby of the manufactured island to find ourselves surrounded by huge crystal chandeliers and golden opulence. This last-minute booking was serendipitous in that it gave my mother and me face time, rather than just talking on the phone.

Not that we were alone on this adventure. There were other people aboard—lots of other people, some of whom I had seen on TV or the Internet, and many, many strangers. The ship held almost 4,000 passengers and crew and most of them seemed to be only a few feet away.

This was a special foodie cruise and it was at capacity. Celebrity chefs from all over the world were aboard for a competition at sea. How I, a lowly food blogger, got an invitation, let alone being fully comped, was beyond me.

We noodled our way through the crowd and took our place in the line to a glass elevator only to be knocked aside as a man rushed between us, recklessly pushing us out of his way.

My mother said, "Well I never...how rude."

I swiveled my head to see who was chasing him and found that he was the one doing the chasing. When he caught up with his quarry he started ranting and waving his arms. His target cowered but I knew I could do nothing to help as they must have known what they signed up for working for famed bombastic chef Miles Stonegate. He had made a career of expressing his outrage at anyone and everyone whom he deemed unworthy, expletives encouraged. To say that I was unhappy the volatile man was on this cruise would be to underbake it.

The elevator doors finally opened and we stuffed ourselves inside. We headed for D deck and the calm of our stateroom.

I looked around for my belongings. "Mom, did they tell us when our luggage would be delivered?"

"It will get here before this evening. Relax, son. There's nothing in your bags you need that they don't already have available."

My mother was a seasoned traveler and cruises were nothing new to her. While I had flown around the world, I had never been on anything like this floating palace.

The Queen Alex 2 wasn't even the biggest ship in the fleet yet she had all the facilities of a small city, from bars and restaurants to nightclubs, show stages, swimming pools, hair salons, gift shops, a casino, and on and on. These were all good things since we were going to be at sea a long time—a week on the open Atlantic with nary a stop till we arrived at Southampton, England.

I sprawled across one of the beds, hanging off three edges—it had been a long day already. Our flights had landed in New York City with plenty of time to get to the port before departure, but no time to spend in the city itself. There were so many restaurants I wanted to review in the Big Apple but it wouldn't happen on this trip. Besides, I would be spending a solid week stuffing myself at the many eateries on board for my blog, along with being a judge for a food competition—something else I had never done before. There were two other judges and very complete rules so I wasn't too concerned about taking on the chore of sampling food created by the greatest chefs from around the world, starting the next morning.

There was a knock at the door. My mother was out on the balcony taking in the view of the Statue of Liberty so I answered. No one was there but our luggage had somehow appeared. I hauled it inside and shouted to my mother that it had arrived.

She came in from the balcony. "We'll be here for a while, so we should unpack and make ourselves at home."

I hoisted our bags onto our beds and looked at the cabin's storage options, of which there were a plethora. Every nook and cranny in our small stateroom offered a shelf or drawer or cabinet to sequester our belongings.

My mother claimed the larger portion of the closet, leaving me two hangers—just enough for my not-so-extensive wardrobe.

She asked, "Are you excited about the competition? Do you think your detective avocation will be helpful for judging?"

"Maybe. But I'm certainly happy to be taking a break from crime-solving. Food and relaxation, and of course plenty of time with my mother are all I'm looking forward to. Nothing but blue skies ahead."

A whistle followed by a voice came over a speaker in the ceiling of our room—we were to find our life preservers and get to a lifeboat right away.

We just got here and we already had to abandon ship?

Chapter Three

"Don't worry," my mother volunteered, apparently sensing my rising anxiety. "They're required to do a lifeboat drill at the beginning of every cruise. I have yet to have had to evacuate."

Several decades in I still reverted to a fearful little boy, cowering behind his mother's apron. "Why do we need the life preservers if it's only a drill?"

"Just follow all the instructions and you'll be fine, son."

I pulled two life preservers from their labeled bin and handed one to my mother. We left our stateroom and heeding directions from the crew, made our way to the lifeboat station—it was a small lobby and not inside an actual lifeboat. I was both relieved and a little disappointed.

Several people had arrived ahead of us and more entered after. A stout man came in and stood next to my mother. I recognized him immediately.

"Big Jim James?" I asked.

"Guilty as charged," he responded, jovially.

"I'm Murph Murphy and this is my mother, Gloria."

"It's so nice to meet you, Mr. James," she said.

"Please call me Jim." He leaned in and kissed the back of her extended hand.

I waited while they had their moment, then interrupted. "Are you one of the competitors? I would really like to taste your famous BBQ."

He said to me, "I'm not sure it's open to the public." To my mother, he said, "But I might be able to get you an invitation."

My mother to the rescue, "My son is one of the judges."

"Then I'll see you both there," he said.

A crew member quieted us down so we could get on with the business at hand. "I'm Lillianalisamarie, the cruise director and I'm in charge of this station. The drill will go quickly if everyone pays attention. We're going to go over how to put on your life preserver and find the way to your lifeboat."

The exercise was kind of like what happens before a plane takes off where the flight attendant gives the safety briefing. Unlike that one, you actually had to pay attention and follow directions before they let you leave. Following directions in this instance was eluding me. The cruise director came over to help adjust my straps.

I wisecracked, "I'm sure this will be much easier when I'm panicking."

"I'll be here to help if the need arises," she assured.

"Thank you. What do people call you for short? Lilli or Lil or…?" I stopped before reciting a full menu of nicknames.

"Lillianalisamarie." She didn't smile.

I may not get that help she promised—best not to need it then. When the drill was over, my mother handed me her life preserver.

"Would you take this back to our room, son? Jim has asked me out for a drink."

"Sure. But don't forget we have early dinner reservations tonight."

Whether she heard me or not I didn't know. She walked off in intense conversation with her new friend. My alone time with my mother was already being subverted.

Chapter Four

I meandered back to the cabin to stow the life preservers where I had found them, ideally never to see them again. Then I went on a walk to locate the casino and see what kind of games were to be had. I was pretty sure any gambling losses wouldn't be comped as part of my gig, but I could stand to lose five bucks at Blackjack.

A sign outside the closed casino said it wouldn't open till we were well out to sea. I would have to find other pre-dinner entertainment.

My phone rang, surprising me—I already felt I had left the real world and things such as cell phones didn't exist here. But we were still docked in New York City after all.

"Mr. Murphy—I'm Monica Hastings, producer of Chefs at Sea," came the voice on the other end. "I wanted to make sure that you made it on board and will be at the production meeting in the morning."

"I'm headed out to the deck to watch us set sail as we speak. I'll be there," I confirmed.

"Very good. Just a friendly reminder—while drinks are included for you and your guest, we do expect judges to be sober."

That was blunt but understandable. "Of course. I'll see you in the morning."

I went out onto an upper deck and leaned on a railing, surveying the shore. The dock slowly slid away. If I hadn't been watching, I wouldn't have been able to tell we were moving at all. People cheered from the pier and the ship.

I gazed down over the railing at the black water swirling far below. Someone brushed behind me and I bolted upright—I was not ready to be tossed into a cold bath.

Manhattan in our wake, the sun began to set over the water. It reflected off the tall, glass buildings and was reminiscent of some of the most beautiful photos of the city I had ever seen. I tipped an imaginary hat to the Statue of Liberty as she faded into the darkness.

Several other brightly-lit cruise ships were exiting the harbor at the same time as us, their passengers likely heading for more exotic destinations than our open ocean journey. I snapped a few shots of the stunning surroundings for the blog and felt my stomach growl. My meal schedule was off and I was ready for dinner.

Chapter Five

My mother had remembered our dinner date and was adding her final jewelry touches in our cabin when I returned. I found my tie and blazer laid out on my bed and took the hint.

I decided we should have dinner in the main dining room the first night. There were so many options for places to eat onboard but, as I understood it, the main dining room was a cruise tradition. I would have plenty of time to try some of the other meal venues during the week-long odyssey.

The hostess ushered us to a six-top with three other guests already seated. The gentlemen at the table stood as my mother and I arrived.

I introduced the two of us as we all sat down. "I'm Murph Murphy and this is my mother, Gloria."

The man next to my mother said, "We're Skyler and Stacy Jones and this is our first cruise."

The speaker did not indicate which of them went with which name. Before I could rectify the situation, the man seated at my side said, "Call me Wells," and reached out to shake my hand.

I obliged and said to the small group, "This is my first cruise, too, though my mother is a frequent voyager. Is this your first cruise, Wells?"

"No," he replied, "I'm well versed in the ways of the sea."

How poetic.

The server appeared at the table and took our drink order. While I had been admonished over the phone not to show up for work drunk, tonight I could imbibe at will. Wells ordered a bottle of Shiraz for the table to get us started. I said I would get the next round. After the wine arrived, menus were presented.

Wells said to us newbies, "If you see something you like on the menu be sure to order it now as much of it changes every night."

I spied many things I might like and was having a tough time deciding. *How would I ask this politely?* "How many things can I order?"

"You can order as much as you want but the mains portions are substantial. Best to stick to the small plates if you want to order several dishes," Wells recommended.

I could do that.

After several small plates, tastes of my mother's food, and two desserts, I decided I'd had enough. I was going to have to pace myself or I wouldn't fit into the tiny stateroom shower by the end of the journey.

My mother got up to excuse herself.

"Are you feeling okay?" I asked. If there was wine left, she was rarely the first away from the table.

"I'm fine. I going to meet Jim at the lobby bar. I'll see you in the room later."

"Um, sure. See you later." I'd wanted to spend time catching up with my mother when I didn't have judge duties, but it seemed Big Jim was more interesting than her son. In actuality, I wouldn't have minded spending time with him myself.

The Jones also bid their adieu, leaving only Wells and myself at the table.

He said, "I'm going to get some fresh air. Care to join me?" He picked up his half-full glass of wine and stood.

I picked up my glass as well and poured the remainder of the bottle into it. "Lead on."

The sun was long gone and the ocean was dark. And then there was the wind, which I had not been expecting. The stiff breeze made it feel that we were racing at a fairly good clip as we left America behind.

Wells found us a couple of deck chairs. Once we sat down below the level of the glass-walled railing, the roar of the wind lessened enough so we could chat.

"How long have you been a food critic?" he asked.

"I started professionally about 15 years ago, though I've been complaining about food as an amateur much longer than that. I did reviews for the local papers and then started my blog, Murphy Slaw."

"Cute. How did you stumble onto this event?"

"I'm not exactly sure. I followed up on a comment on my blog that I thought was a bad joke. Before I knew it, tickets were in my email and I was on a plane to NY."

"With your mother in tow?" He raised his eyebrows.

"The tickets were for two and we rarely get to see each other so I thought it might be fun. How did you hear about this cruise?"

"I was invited as well—being top in my field."

It was then I realized whom I had been spending the evening with. "Oh, nuts. You're Welland Goode. You have something like four five-star restaurants. I'm sorry I didn't recognize you."

"Five, actually. But no matter."

"I went to Akorn the last time I was in San Francisco. It was the best vegan meal I've ever had."

He smiled wide, "Thank you. We try very hard to ensure even carnivores get a satisfying meal."

"It was way more than satisfying. If I wasn't contractually committed to eating every animal put on a plate in front of me, I think I could be sated just eating food from Akorn."

"That's quite a compliment."

I swigged down the rest of my wine and set the glass on a nearby table as I stood. "Unfortunately, I have an early meeting and had better get some rest. I'll see you there?"

"Will you?" he asked.

"I'm one of the judges."

"Interesting. Then I'll see you in the morning." He took another sip of his wine.

I left him behind, walking off in the wrong direction, and waved at him sheepishly as I came by a second time after correcting course.

Finding our cabin empty, I surmised my mother was not yet back from her date.

I got ready for bed and then tried to figure out how to get online. I had to let my blog readers know I was out to sea.

Chapter Six

My mother was sleeping soundly in the other bed when I woke. I had no idea how late she had come in so I did my best not to wake her.

I pillaged a bounteous breakfast buffet on the way to my meeting—it was time to earn my keep.

The aft end of a large dining hall had been commandeered and repurposed into a television production studio. There were several cameras, lots of lights, and TV crew running everywhere. Along the back was a jumble of cooking stations. To one side there were café tables and chairs for a limited number of audience members, who were not present. A table with three chairs was located along the other side with a table card that read, "Judges." I guessed that was my mark and took the middle seat.

The competitors were still working their way to their chairs at a long table in the center of the room. I knew who some of the chefs were. Square in the middle of the table sat Big Jim. Next to him was Wells. I recognized a French chef but couldn't recall his name. There would be introductions soon enough. I was relieved that surly Miles Stonegate was nowhere in sight.

Near the end of the long table was a man with a bad case of resting pickle face. I didn't know if he had been shanghaied onto this cruise or if he was happy as a clam and merely looked like there were a dozen flies in his chowder.

Seated at the other end of the table was a young man in board shorts and a t-shirt, almost absorbed into his phone. He wasn't dressed in a crisp chef's uniform like the rest.

What was his story? It wasn't long till I found out.

A woman bent down and whispered to him. He got up and came over to sit next to me at the judge's table.

His phone still commanded his attention and I could now see he was on level 11 of some shooter. I so wanted to interrupt him but kept my cool. He looked vaguely familiar but was out of place. You know like when you run into someone in the grocery store you recognize but you're not sure from where, even though they've been your postal person for years? It was like that. I'd seen him before, but not in the food world.

The third and final judge took the seat on the other side of me. Her I recognized. It was too late for me to stand courteously while she sat down as I had been focused on the gamer. I reached out my hand to shake hers and she tenuously accepted. Before I could commit a second *faux pas*, a woman at the front of the room spoke into a microphone for the save.

"Ladies and gentlemen, it's time we got started. I want to welcome you all to the first day of Chefs at Sea."

There was a smattering of applause from the competitors and us judges.

She continued, "I'm the producer, Monica Hastings. We've invited chefs from all over the world to demonstrate their culinary skills and prove who is the best chef at sea, as determined by our three judges." She motioned toward the contestants, and then us. "I would like to introduce our host of Chefs at Sea—he's a chef in his own right, has had his own television shows, and has hosted many cooking competitions.

Judges, chefs, please give a warm round of applause to Declan Beige."

Declan Beige! I had no idea he was going to be here. I would have to work even harder not to embarrass myself.

He came out from behind a curtained-off area and took a gracious bow to the applauding assembly, then quickly retreated behind the curtain, likely to continue preparing for the show.

Monica spoke again, "Chefs, I would like to introduce our esteemed judges—renowned chef and cookbook author Avery Penfield, actor Cole Robby, and from the online world Murph Murphy."

So, Cole was an actor. That was probably why he looked familiar to me, even though I couldn't think of what I might have seen him in.

Monica gave us all the rundown on how the competition was to work. As could be guessed, the chefs would cook and the judges judge. The judging was to be blind so we couldn't be there for the actual meal prep. In fact, as soon as we were told that lunch would be the first battle, we were dismissed right away. I had been looking forward to watching and learning from the skilled chefs, but that was not to be.

As Avery, Cole, and I had never met, I suggested we adjourn to one of the lounges to get to know each other. Avery ordered hot, black tea while Cole ordered a soda. My espresso came strong and diminutive.

Avery began, "Mr. Murphy, exactly what is the 'online world'?"

She was just as formal and starchy in person as she was on other shows where I had seen her judge.

"Well," I began, "I have a food blog, Murphy Slaw."

"Is this what the world is coming to?" She seemed unimpressed.

I observed, "The judges seem to have been chosen from the popular forms of media. Me from the Internet, yourself from books and TV, and Cole here, from the big screen."

At the sound of his name, Cole came up for air from his game. He took a long drag on his soda straw.

Avery asked us, "Have either of you ever judged a competition at this level before?"

Cole and I shook our heads. I noted that Avery should have inquired if we had judged at any level before.

"So, Cole, what brings you here?" I asked.

"My agent made me come." He took another drag on his soda straw.

"What?"

"She thought it would be good for my career—make me seem more friendly and approachable or something. I don't even like food."

I doubled down, "What?"

Avery groaned. "I'm the only proper judge here? I'm going to my flat."

As she strutted off, I said to Cole, "But your job is literally to eat."

"That's always been a job to me. I do it 'cause I have to, not because I want to."

That explained the contrast in our belt sizes.

He said, "I'm an actor. I'll act like I'm tasting the food and make a good or bad face."

"But you will have to actually taste it so you can vote. People will be able to tell if you don't put the food into your mouth."

"The camera can pan away as I lift my fork. We do it all the time."

Avery might have been on the right track. This could be a disaster. "Perhaps I can teach you a few things?"

"No thanks. I'm good."

He may be good, but I was imagining rough seas ahead for the rest of us. "I've never judged before either, but I can tell you what to do, as far as tastings go."

He looked back to his game. "It's TV. You read your lines and I'll read mine."

"Read your lines?"

"Yeah, from the script. Duh."

It could have gone worse, but I wasn't sure how. "There's no script."

"There's always a script. All these reality shows are fake."

He was right, to a point. "As I understand it, there's a production script for the show, but there are no lines for us to read."

"Then how do we know what to say?"

"We taste the food and say what we think about it."

He didn't look up from his game. "What's there to say about food? I just eat it when I have to. I don't think about it."

"You can say things about it being too salty or sweet and whether you like it or not."

"What kind of food will there be?" He shot me a concerned look. It seemed as if he had never seen a cooking show before, which, given his disgust at actually having to eat to survive, would be expected.

"It could be anything—trout pizza, a duck hoagie, spaghetti pie, or even toad in the hole."

I could smell his fear. My examples may have been a little too extreme, though I have certainly been served more exotic dishes than those.

"I can't eat any of that! I need to text my agent. I'm not doing this."

"Wait, wait. I have no idea what they'll prepare for us. You can get through it. You give it a taste and move on to the next dish."

"The next dish?"

I wasn't making things better. "Each of the chefs will have something for us to try."

"I can't do it."

"You absolutely can do it. Look at this as a chance to expand your world. Food is the crux of everything. It's more than how we power ourselves. It's something we can savor. Enjoy. Share with friends."

"I don't have any friends here. My agent was supposed to come, but…" He sounded a little glum.

"You have a friend now. I'll help you as much as you'll let me. Perhaps you can help me out, too. The producer said we need to come in early for hair and makeup. How early do you think I should be?"

"I'm planning for 10 minutes." He noisily slurped up the rest of his soda. "You might want to give them 30."

Was that a diss? "You would think with a name like Cole Robby, food would be in your DNA."

"What does that mean?" He didn't wait for an answer and got up. "I need a drink."

"I'll buy." I thought it best to keep my eye on him as there was that whole thing about staying sober for the show.

Chapter Seven

I needn't have worried about Cole spending the rest of the morning getting sloshed as he ordered an energy drink. Avery, however, was a different story. I noticed her in the bar, rather than going to her cabin as she had promised, and the drink in front of her looked positively toxic. She didn't see me and I thought it best to keep it that way.

As I had nothing pressing to do for a couple of hours, I took a walk around my floating home to get the lay of the land, so to speak. I found a small library that was empty save for one other man and offered a wind-free view of the water. And that was all there was to see out the window—water, water everywhere—no land or other ships in sight.

It was still early and the deck outside was deserted, until a movement in the distance caught my eye. The creature was small and furry and scurrying my way along the deck.

There are rats on this barge!

It kept running towards me but I was safely inside—it couldn't get in here, could it? Wait. It wasn't a rat. The not-rat stopped in front of my window and barked once at me.

"Murphy?" I couldn't believe it. How could Murphy be way out here?

The other man had joined me at the window as the wee beast turned and continued his jaunt along the deck.

"Do you know that dog?" he asked, in an accent that wasn't quite British.

"I think so, but I can't see how it's possible. In any case, somebody should be told there's a dog loose onboard before he falls over the side or gets into some other trouble."

"I'll take care of it." The man ran off in the same direction as the dog.

He returned shortly. "We caught him and a crew member is taking him back to the kennel. What makes you think he's this Murphy you mentioned?"

I was still staring out the window along the deck looking for more rats. When I turned to face the man, I was caught speechless. I was mesmerized by his eyes—they were the most unique color of green I had ever seen—the color of the greenest pistachios.

"Sir?" he prodded.

"I'm so sorry," I stammered. "I've just never seen..." I was finally able to look away from his eyes and try to compose myself.

He tossed me a life preserver, "My mum's were even greener, if you can imagine that. So, about the dog? There has to be a heap of dogs that look exactly like that one. Why do you think you know him?"

"It's just a feeling I have—a foreboding feeling. Are pets even allowed onboard?"

"On most cruises, no, other than service animals. But this ship has a kennel with about a dozen dogs on this trip. The dogs aren't supposed to be on the loose—I don't know how he got out. By the way, I'm Arthur."

"Nice to meet you. I'm Murph Murphy."

"Murphy—like the dog?" He looked a bit confused.

"It's a long story," I said.

"I have a few minutes before I have to get to rehearsal," he prompted.

"There's this woman," I started.

"Girlfriend?"

I disputed the inference, "She's just a friend. Or not even a friend—more of a stalker, really. I'm a food blogger and she says she's my biggest fan. Anyway, Murphy is her dog. She never goes anywhere without him."

"You think this woman..."

I filled in his blank, "Kimber. Kimberly Wilson."

"You think Ms. Wilson is on board?"

"Given her history with me, I've got a bad feeling. Something terrible always happens when she's around."

Chapter Eight

My phone blipped—time to go judge. I made my way to the makeshift studio. I was the last to arrive at the judges' table—hair and makeup took a little longer than I thought it should. The seven competitors, unfortunately including Miles Stonegate, were all seated at their table watching us. Audience members and TV cameras were watching us, too. I felt a little uncomfortable with all this attention. People usually viewed my blog videos when I wasn't around.

I took a moment to breathe. The studio had had what I could only describe as a general boat smell at the morning meeting. Now there were so many competing scents of everything from coffee to garlic to fryer grease—the chefs had been very busy.

I wondered how Cole was doing. I knew he was used to the attention but I was sure he was dreading what was coming—food, strange food. I wanted to say something to soothe his nerves but the host, Declan Beige, got things started before I had the chance.

"Let's welcome our judges—Avery Penfield, Cole Robby, and Murph Murphy."

Declan Beige said my name!

The audience applauded politely. We nodded to our adoring fans, well Avery and Cole's adoring fans, anyway. I was sure most of them had no idea who I was. But no matter—they were here to see the famous chefs and sample their dishes, as were we.

"Judges, our chefs have been cooking for you all morning," Declan said. "It's time to taste their lunch creations and decide whose dish is best and who will walk the plank."

The small crowd laughed at the high-seas humor.

"Our first dish is jerk pork with sea-salt pineapple. Audience, there is a sample of each dish for you as well so that you may taste and vote along with our judges, but you must remain silent."

I glanced over at Cole as the plates were set in front of us. At least we were off to an easy start for him, just pork and fruit.

He saw me looking at him and leaned over to me. "I didn't get my script. Can I look at yours?"

"Cole, there are no scripts. You have to taste the food and tell us what you think."

He did not look happy. "What is this?"

"It's spicy pork. You can do this. Just give it a small taste." I picked up a piece of pork on my fork and demonstrated popping it into my mouth and then chewing.

He shot me a scowl and started to pick up a forkful of pig. I reached out and grabbed his arm to stop him.

"Am I doing it wrong?" he asked.

I released him and took a big slug of water. "No, I want to warn you—it's spicy. I mean really spicy. So spicy I'm not sure I'll be able to taste any of the other dishes." I quickly forked a piece of the pineapple and stuffed it into my mouth. It helped soothe the burn, at least more than the water.

Cole sat frozen, fork halfway to his mouth.

"I have an idea," I whispered to him. "Take a small piece of the pork and a big piece of pineapple at the same time. That should help with the spice level." I tested the combination and it did provide the needed balance.

"I can't do that," he whispered back at me.

"Why not?"

"I can't eat different foods that are touching."

It was going to be a long competition.

"Then at least start small," I warned.

He took a tiny bite of the pork and immediately spit it into his napkin. "Okay, I'm done," he announced.

"You have to at least try the pineapple. It's not spicy."

He bit off a piece of it. "It's salty and sweet." He even offered a small smile. I hoped the cameras got that because it might be the best they get from him for the entire show.

Avery and I made a few notes on the pads in front of us as the next dish arrived.

The crew juggled tall white-bread towers on plates as they served the audience members.

What in the world?

Even taller towers finally came to each of us at the judges' table.

The host explained, "Next up is a finger sandwich of cucumber and crème fraîche."

This was a finger sandwich?

Declan had to be messing with us. It included crustless white bread with a filling between, but it was composed of multiple levels each a little smaller than the last to form something approximating the Eiffel Tower. It was so tall that four celery-stick buttresses were used to keep it from toppling. And there were toothpicks—so many toothpicks—holding it all together. Toothpicked to the very top was a green olive stuffed with a red pimento.

Cole elbowed me gently. "How do we eat this?"

"I don't know. I've never seen anything like it. It's too tall to get a knife through and knocking it over will make a mess on the table."

I looked to our more seasoned judge and saw her turning her plate as if one of the other identical sides would offer an answer. I scoped out the audience for a bit of crowdsourced help. It seemed that most had started from the top and were working their way down. Good enough for me—I dug in.

Cole, after watching me, tossed the olive to the floor behind him then lifted the topmost, smallest sandwich off of his tower and gingerly took a bite.

It was an okay finger sandwich, but nothing special, other than the presentation, which had apparently consumed all of the chef's time, not leaving any to get creative with the innards. The question was whether the presentation was a plus or a minus. Searching out all the toothpicks so as not to get skewered in my soft palate sent it to the minus column for me.

Several more dishes came and went without fanfare. The final dish was pumpkin cardamom soup. It seemed the chef wasn't sure whether it was best served hot or cold as it was in a split bowl with one side hot and one side chilled. The hot side may have had more pepper, or maybe the cold version dulled my tongue, but I could taste neither pumpkin nor cardamom on either half.

After the final dish was cleared, Declan came back on the scene. "Time for judging the first round. Our team of esteemed judges will determine the best dish, along with the dish of the first chef who will exit the competition. The audience has been given cards to fill in with their favorite and least favorite dish as well. Audience, please do that now and then pass the cards in."

The three of us at the judging table conferred. Cole didn't like much of it but found the soup tolerable when hot, and of course, the toothpick sandwich was okay with him. We had our winner and loser. We nodded to the producer who then motioned to the crew.

An example of each dish was set on the table in front of the chef who created it.

Avery had been chosen to deliver the news of the winning dish for this round. "The best lunch we were served today was...," she paused for effect, or possibly a future commercial break—she had done this before, "...the jerk pork and pineapple."

There was a smattering of applause from the audience as Big Jim stood behind his dish at the competitors' table. While I hadn't tried to guess whose dish was whose during judging, he was the king of meat. The overabundance of spice had almost lost it for him, though.

My turn. "And the dish that did not make the cut—the sandwich tower. I'm sorry but it was too difficult to eat for little reward."

The British chef, Miles Stonegate, stood behind his sandwich tower scowling at me. He finally smiled at the camera and thanked everyone for the extra time he would now have to enjoy his cruise home. And I would not have to face him for the rest of the competition, so it was win-win—or actually lose-win in this case.

The audience votes were tallied and they also liked the jerk pork the best but weren't soup fans.

Declan put a bow on it. "Thank you all for coming to this first round of Chefs at Sea. We will adjourn until tomorrow when the chefs will be cooking brunch for our judges and one more competitor will be eliminated. We'll see you all then."

Monica the producer immediately stopped by our table. "You don't need to be here until about 11 tomorrow. I'll send you a message when we're ready. Thank you each for the good work today."

So my next day's meal schedule would be breakfast followed by brunch. I couldn't hate that if I tried.

Chapter Nine

I found my mother reading in our stateroom.

"Where shall we go for dinner tonight?" I asked. "Did you want to go back to the main dining room or try one of the specialty restaurants?"

"I'm sorry, son. Big Jim is taking me to the Korean place tonight to celebrate his first win. I would invite you to join but the reservation is only for two."

"I'm sure you would. He's not wasting any time, is he? Don't worry about me. I've made a career of eating by myself."

"How was the cookoff today?" she asked.

"The food wasn't all that great. I hope they up their games for tomorrow."

It was too early for dinner so I cruised by the casino to try to get rid of some cash that I had only been keeping around to pay bills. This time the sign said it was closed for cleaning. There seemed to be a conspiracy to keep me from being separated from my wallet. There were still many days left on this journey—they couldn't hide from me forever.

I checked the ship's schedule and found that pickleball had started. I didn't know what it was, but I did like pickles. I had only had breakfast, lunch, and second lunch on the show, such as it was, so a light snack before dinner seemed in order.

I found the sports deck and saw people swinging paddles at a whiffle ball—pickleball was exercise! No pickles in sight, I found a server and ordered a drink while I sat nearby. My dirty martini showed up as I had ordered it—vodka and vermouth with pickle brine in place of olive brine as my contribution to the match.

While I didn't know the rules of the game I was watching, one of the four players certainly acted as if he was losing, stomping around the court and letting his partner know in no uncertain terms of his frustration. I was pleased to see the British chef who had lost the first round venting at someone other than me, though I felt bad for his partner, the pickle-faced chef.

Chapter Ten

Another day, another chance to get all judgy. My phone blipped just before 11—time for the second round of tasting. I'd made sure to have a hearty breakfast earlier that morning in case the chefs' brunch offerings were subpar.

I joined Cole at the judges' table. Avery was nowhere to be seen and the producer looked nervous.

"I wasn't sure I'd see you today," I said to Cole.

"I talked to my agent last night and she said I couldn't quit. It would get out to the tabloids and I'd be a laughing stock."

"You should be okay today—I think brunch might be the safest meal for you. You do eat eggs?"

"Yeah, though I don't like them all squishy."

Avery came in and made a beeline for the producer. She looked like she'd been windsurfing behind the ship. The producer glanced at Cole and me before sending Avery off with the makeup person. It seemed we would have some extra time before we got started.

I wanted to spend some of it talking to Big Jim about what was up with him and my mother, but I thought better of speaking with a competitor before judging. It might look bad, or I could inadvertently get tipped off as to who had made what.

Cole had pulled out his phone and was now on level 23 of his game. I went to talk to the producer.

"What's up with Avery?" I asked.

Monica looked toward the competitors' table and quickly back at me. "There's nothing you need to know, Murph. We'll be all set to start in a few minutes."

What was that all about? Avery was a mess and Monica wouldn't fill me in. I must be losing my touch.

Avery was composed and back at our table shortly.

Declan Beige kicked off the tourney. "Welcome to the second day of Chefs at Sea.

Today, the remaining chefs have created brunch dishes. As always audience, please stay quiet while you taste each of the dishes along with our judges."

Among the offerings were waffles, pancakes, and eggs—some squishy. Cole separated each element of each dish and gave what he could a taste. I was somewhat proud of him—or perhaps it was his agent I should thank.

Several dishes in, Declan announced, "This chef presents Eggs Offal on Frico."

The reddish-grey pile of scrambled eggs had stowed away on a raft of crisped yellow cheese. I hesitated to look over at Cole. This would be way past his comfort zone.

He leaned over to me. "Why are the eggs called awful? They look funny but why serve them if they're not good?"

How would I put this? There was no satisfactory way to describe offal to Cole, or most people, for that matter—organ meat can be off-putting. While I was stalling, he poked at them and put a small sample into his mouth. I would never be able to tell him what he had eaten after that.

He didn't look happy, but he didn't spit them out either.

"They taste meaty, but like metal."

"I imagine they would." I had to use my imagination because I hadn't quite gotten around to tasting them myself. "Try the frico underneath them. It's cooked cheese."

He broke off a bit of the lacey cheese raft and scraped the egg matter away. Tasting that earned me a smile and nod, not that I had anything to do with the dish.

Avery announced, "This looks like the dog's dinner," and pushed her plate away.

Next, we were served what Declan assured us was a bagel and lox. The bagel was open-face and lacked the traditional capers, red onion, and even any lox. There was only a schmear of plain, white cream cheese on the bagel, a lonely sprig of dill perched on top. I looked back and forth at the other judge's plates, wondering if the chef had run out of time and I had been short-changed, but they were all the same.

"Cole, did you get any lox?" I asked.

"I don't think so. But I don't know what it is."

"It's Jewish bacon."

"It is?" Cole dove right in.

Avery shrugged and took a bite. I did the same. It tasted like a bagel and lox with capers and onion.

What trickery was this?

Avery made notes while I poked at the cream cheese to see if there was lox hiding somewhere. And there was. It was baked into the bagel! This mad chef had not only made his own bagels but he had snuck capers, red onions, and chunks of lox into them. I could now see why the dish looked so plain—you wouldn't want to distract from this kind of genius.

I looked across at the chefs who were all stone-faced, not to give it away. Who could have done this? And why have I never eaten this before?

Cole had nearly finished his bagel. I was amazed. I started to tell him what was up but thought better of it. He was enjoying foods that he didn't know were touching.

The round soon ended and we had to eliminate another competitor. I knew who my winner was and Cole voted along with me, overriding Avery's choice of black pudding benedict. The man with the bad case of resting pickle face, Canadian chef Ken Gemani, stood proudly behind his bagel creation, a big smile making him look much more approachable.

The losing dish of Eggs Offal on Frico sent the Italian chef packing.

The host set us free after telling everyone that next up would be the dessert round.

Should I rush out to see if the casino was open? No, I still wanted to talk to Big Jim. As I had suspected, the steak and somewhat squishy eggs, the audience's favorite, had been his. It had been well-executed—I ranked it above the black pudding—but it couldn't beat out the bagel for creativity. I found Big Jim sampling a bagel for himself.

"So, Big Jim," I started, "you and my mother, huh?"

He wiped some cream cheese from the corner of his mouth with the sleeve of his jacket. "I hope that's not a problem for you. Your mother is a fine lady. I'm sure our relationship wouldn't be cause for you to vote me off the show." He winked at me.

"Just the opposite. Voting you out would merely give you more time to spend with my mother. The only time she has for me now is when you're cooking."

"Then I must be a shoo-in to win," he chuckled.

"You're good, but you do have some competition. I wouldn't slack off if I were you. Say, you don't know what was up with Avery, do you? Monica wouldn't tell me anything but I think she looked your way when I asked."

"I don't think she was looking at me. But there may be another chef involved. I can't say."

"You can't say or you won't say?" I prodded.

"C'mon Murph. I'm sure you know there are many secrets a chef has to keep. Whatever is going on between two consenting adults won't affect the competition. Look, I've got a date tonight. I can't show up in these smelly chef's rags."

"I don't suppose you can." It sounded like I would be having dinner by myself, again.

Big Jim left me alone with my thoughts. "Secrets," he had said. Did Avery's secrets matter? She was a professional. And it was blind judging, though her friend, or lover, could tip her off. But he, or she, would have to have a dish good enough to convince me or Cole to play along, too. And if that were the case, perhaps they deserved the win.

Chapter Eleven

Monica had arranged for everyone involved in Chefs at Sea to get a guided tour of the ship's main kitchen. I had been in the cookhouses of innumerable restaurants, but none that served the sheer volume of meals that were required every day on the QA2.

I met up with our group at one of the galley entrances. Dressed down to their street clothes, the "star" chefs looked like any other passenger on the ship.

I didn't see Wells whom I'd had dinner with the first night in the group but the first contestant voted off the show found me right away.

"Hello, Mr. Murphy. I'm sorry you were so distressed by my dish," he said, British sarcasm not held back. At least Chef Miles Stonegate wasn't yelling at me—yet.

"I wouldn't say I was distressed. It was just too much form over function. If it was simply an edible table display, it would have been a lovely addition." I tried to be as diplomatic as possible. Knowing his temperament, there was no reason to antagonize him further, for either of our sakes.

The tour guide quieted us down and led us through the galley doors. Chef Miles stayed close, keeping me ill at ease.

The kitchen was like many I had been in but on a much grander scale. All of the cooking pots were huge. Everything was stainless steel, and I mean everything. The work tables, the soup cookers, the sinks, even the floors and ceilings were covered in polished metal. Our tour guide explained to us that it made it easier to keep clean and food safe. There was even an entirely separate area for meat so that no fruits or vegetables could be contaminated. Nobody wanted food poisoning.

All the while the British chef stayed nearby—it didn't seem as though he was through with me. He had been the first voted off the show—a humiliating position to be in.

Did failed contestants on these shows often go after a judge? Was revenge a thing?

I could have pointed out to him that it was at least a split decision, having only been Avery and I that had voted him off, overruling Cole who could somehow eat a sandwich even though everything was touching everything else. He thought the stereotypical bland British meal was the best one that he had been forced to eat, so far.

The tour soon ended with no further conflict and one final fact—an impressive 65,000 eggs are consumed over the duration of a cruise.

Chapter Twelve

This day's Chefs at Sea would be all about dessert. I loaded up on protein at both breakfast and an early lunch to try to bypass the almost-certainly upcoming sugar rush.

I had spent the morning in between meals updating my blog from one of the pool-adjacent hot tubs. I wasn't allowed to let the cat out of the bag as to who had won a round and who had already been shown the door, but I could post some general musings.

I arrived at the judge's table first for a change. Avery soon joined and gave me a pleasant, though fake, smile. She didn't seem to be my biggest fan. She visibly deflated when Cole took his seat on the other side of me.

First up for judging was a Pavlova in the shape of a life preserver ring that looked like it had washed up on a beach many years ago and had yellowed in the sun. *Could that have been the effect the chef was looking for?*

It was sliced up and served to us and the audience and was an overly saccharine starting dish, with undertones of lemon and possibly mustard. Stuffed with strips of candied lemon peel, and corn chips, I was pretty sure—or at least hoped—we had already found our last-place dish.

Our host introduced our next treat. "This dessert has an ocean resonance—a take on a salted caramel cupcake served with lobster butter ice cream. You'll find a cinnamon cupcake topped by a chile-caramel buttercream frosting and crowned with *ikura*—salmon roe—to provide saltiness."

And indeed, that was what I found—a neat stack of orange roe had been carefully placed on top of each cupcake. It was delicious—a little heat, a little salt, a little umami. Cole ate around the salmon roe—he was missing out.

I noted he'd quickly emptied his ice cream bowl—a good call. The velvety, buttery frozen delight was a great foil to the spicy cupcake and was something I would love to find at my local ice creamery.

After a passable tart, our penultimate entry was a nut brittle that had bacon in it. Big Jim's fingerprints were all over this one and I did not look his way as I didn't want confirmation. The pecans, cashews, almonds, and peanuts each brought their own subtleties, almost, but not quite, overshadowed by bacon in every bite. It was sweet and toffee-like with a smoky, subtlety burned quality that was perfect. At the tail end was a bit of red pepper spice, letting you know it was far above any peanut brittle you had ever eaten. I could go on and on but I guess I already did.

Declan wheeled out the final dessert on a cart. "And now I present a tossed salad in a handmade mahogany bowl."

Cole and I exchanged questioning glances.

"Come now judges," Declan continued, "salad is served after the main in many parts of the world."

Of course, he was right—was he ever wrong? But it was still unexpected in a dessert challenge.

"I shall serve." He pulled out a long knife, cut down the center, and clean through the bowl as the knowing audience oohed and aahed.

It was cake! But it was a dry cake, the modeling chocolate lettuce and other vegetable copycats not able to provide needed moisture.

I had a tough decision between the seafood duo and the brittle for my winner. Cole voted for the brittle—bacon, and Avery's vote went to the cupcake and ice cream. I agreed with her that the pair was a bit more unique. We all concurred the Pavlova creator could go home.

As was customary for the show, a sample of each dish was brought out and set in front of the chefs. Wells, looked very pleased, and rightly so, having created the cupcake with ice cream, and Big Jim, as expected, had cooked up the nut brittle.

So far, Big Jim, Ken, and Wells had each won a challenge. Three days of competition left it was still anybody's game, with appetizers up next.

Chapter Thirteen

There was a different show in the QA2's main theatre every night. The previous night had been a musical extravaganza. This evening there was a variety show with comedy, music, and magic.

As I entered the large, ornate theatre I spotted Avery sitting in the crowd. I made my way to one of the last seats, across the room from her. Good thing my mother had other plans as I didn't see a pair of empty seats together anywhere in the house. These evening shows were very popular.

The cruise director, Lillianalisamarie, introduced our emcee for the evening, Roo deDay. Tall and sleek, and dressed to the hilt, she swept onto the stage to great applause.

"Thank you. Thank you all. I'd like to invite my co-conspirator to the stage. Please welcome Misti Moor!"

The crowd burst into more applause as the two fabulously-dressed women held hands and bowed to us.

"How are you enjoying your cruise, Misti?" Roo posed.

"I have to admit I'm a bit afraid of being so far out in the ocean," Misti replied.

"So you're Chicken of the Sea?"

The audience groaned fittingly.

"I heard that you've been unhappy as well," Misti returned.

"It's true. I was very upset about the tiny closet in my inside stateroom."

An audience member whooped in agreement.

Roo continued, "There was no room for all my pretty dresses, but I'm good now."

"What happened?" Misti asked.

"The captain sent me to a hanger management class."

Roo turned back to the again groaning audience. "I hope everyone is having a magical cruise. To add to that, here's Marvelous Mac!"

Roo motioned to one of the wings but no one came onstage.

A small voice said, "I'm back here."

The two women parted and there stood a magician who had miraculously appeared behind them. Roo shook his hand as if this was perfectly normal and she and Misti proceeded offstage.

"Hi, everybody! I am indeed Marvelous Mac, here to entertain you with sorcery and other mind games. But first, I'll need help from someone in the audience." He pointed to a person in the front row. "You, sir. Would you please join me on stage?"

The man complied.

"What is your name, sir, and where are you from?"

"Skyler Jones and I'm from Boston."

At least that mystery was solved.

"I never would have known from that accent."

The audience tittered.

Mac positioned Skyler so the audience could see them both. "I have a game I'd like to play with you—it's called 1, 2, 3. We've never met, correct?"

"That is true."

"Let me get into your head—not physically as that would be too messy." Mac the magician closed his eyes. "1 grand piano, 2 dogs, and 3 children."

The man nodded and the audience cheered. He returned to his seat.

"Do we have another victim, I mean customer?" Mac asked. "You, sir, in the red—what is that—a blazer? It certainly looks like it's ablaze."

French chef Alain Lacqua stood and was escorted onto the stage as the spectators applauded.

"1 mortgage, 2 ex-wives, and 3 red jackets like this one." Mac motioned at the man's coat.

The audience roared as the man flashed them a broad smile along with his jacket's bright yellow lining before returning to his seat.

Mac pointed to another of the chefs in the audience, Welland Goode.

Wells shook his head. "No one is sharing my secrets."

The man hadn't seemed shy to me, but he also might not embrace the moment as the French chef had.

The show continued with more comedy, magic, and a few musical interludes, with Roo and Misti finally bidding us a fond farewell.

Chapter Fourteen

The fourth day of the competition the weather turned on us. No longer warm and sunny, the sky was menacing and the cold wind could slice through a tough roast. White caps covered the sea but the Queen Alex 2 was steady.

Pro tip: Get a cabin near the middle of the ship to minimize any turbulence.

That day's cookoff round was appetizers—so many unappetizing appetizers.

Had the chefs turned on us like the weather?

The host first introduced us to Hades on Horseback, Extreme Edition. I shuddered at Declan's explanation, "Bacon wrapped around a prune wrapped around a jalapeno wrapped around a kalamata olive stuffed with blue cheese."

Cole immediately began deconstructing it. I was tempted to follow his lead but bit into it complete. All the flavors were muddied with salt as the overwhelming note.

The next plate comprised of a large roasted Brussels sprout in a purplish sauce Declan described as made from "pureed Ube—a purple yam, Yuzu, and fish sauce." A hole through the sprout hosted a sardine, its head poking out one side and its tail the other.

Cole looked at his plate from which the sardine was looking back at him and quickly got up and made for the exit.

Avery muttered, "Oh, for heaven's sake. Can't we just tuck in?"

I jumped up and followed Cole out while members of the small audience murmured to each other. I caught up with him at the bar as he was calling the bartender over. I waved the barkeep off.

"You can't be drinking during the show," I said to Cole.

"This time I'm done for good. Did you see that...that...?"

"I did and I think it saw me, too."

"And you're going to eat it?" He was visibly shaking.

"That's our job. Look, it's just a vegetable and a small, cooked fish. You can separate them if you like."

"But it has a head."

"It does have a head but you don't have to eat that part, or the tail either, for that matter. You made it through Hades on Horseback." I noted that he had tasted a couple of the separated ingredients.

"But…bacon."

I agreed that bacon fixed a lot of problems. "You've come a long way. You can at least try the Brussels sprout and give an honest opinion, good or bad. Don't let the fish win. There's only one dish left to try after this one—it can't be any worse, right?"

"Can't it? And there are still more days of this to come. This was a bad idea."

"You're an actor, right?" I had my own, possibly bad, idea.

"Yeah."

"Have you ever been in an awful show?"

"Yeah."

"Did you quit before the end?" I hoped he hadn't or my plan was toast.

"No. I did the job I signed up for."

"Then turn that little fish so that he stares down the chefs and give the dish a taste."

I ushered him back to the studio and we took our seats.

Avery sniped, "Can we crack on?"

Monica got everybody settled down and we picked up the show where we had left off. Cole pulled the fish from its burrow and laid it on his plate facing the chefs.

The final appetizer wasn't worse than the fish, but dried fruit and mascarpone with chopped walnuts on crackers certainly wasn't inspired. Maybe the chef's original menu plan had failed.

It was hard to pick a winner—none of the appetizers rose to the level of making anyone want seconds or even firsts. As judges, we had to put up with that kind of abuse, but the poor studio audience shouldn't have had to go along for this ride. We gave up and selected the cracker as the least offensive dish—in other words, the winner. The French chef got lucky that day.

Picking the losing dish was no easier—there were many contenders for it. In the end, the Brussels sprout dish was chosen and Chef Ken's pickle face would no longer be seen in the competition.

Before turning us loose, Declan announced that next time the chefs would prepare holiday dinners.

Just what we needed—bigger meals.

My judge duties for the day complete, I needed a pit stop but a shortcut outside would be unwise. The weather had worsened during the cookoff round and sheets of rain assaulted the windows. After zigzagging through the ship to get back to my cabin, I found an envelope on the outside of my door—an invitation, actually.

Chapter Fifteen

The card inside the envelope I found on our cabin door was a request that my mother and I join the captain at his table for the formal dinner that evening. I let myself into our room and stood staring into the closet. I saw nothing suitable for a formal dinner with the captain—nothing on my side of the closet, anyway. My mother's side, on the other hand, displayed many beautiful gowns, any of which would be appropriate.

There was a knock at the door and I let my mother in.

"Oh, good, you're here. I forgot my key," she said.

"We have a huge problem," I returned.

"It's only a key. The cabin steward would have let me in if you weren't here."

"No. That's not it." I showed her the invitation. "You know I don't own a tuxedo, or even a decent suit, for that matter." I was hoping my mother would tell me everything would be alright if I wore my nicest slacks. She did not.

"An invitation to the captain's table is a great honor, son. You must look your best. They have a tuxedo rental shop onboard. Let me find my key and we'll get you polished up."

I had never worn a tuxedo in my life, not even at my weddings. That should've given my ex-wives an idea of what to expect, I supposed.

Out of all the actual celebrities on board, why in the world would the captain want to have dinner with me?

At least I would finally get to have a night out with my mother.

Chapter Sixteen

My mother and I were escorted to the captain's table. She was seated on one side of the captain's empty, oversized chair with me next to her. The chair on the far side of the captain's was occupied by someone who should have been unexpected but was not.

"Hi, Murph," she waved. "Hello, Mrs. Murphy." She reached out her hand to my mother.

"Mother, this is Kimberly Wilson. And it's not 'Murphy,' Kimber. She's remarried since my father."

"Please call me Gloria and it's nice to meet you, Kimberly. Are you part of the cooking show my son is here for?"

"No, though I am friends with the producer."

"You!" I exclaimed.

"*Moi?*" she responded, innocently.

"You're the reason I'm here. You got me onto the show."

"Did I?"

Wells was brought over by a hostess and sat next to me.

"Mother, you remember Wells from dinner the first night," I said.

He reached over and shook her extended hand. "Lovely to see you again."

"And this is Kimberly Wilson," I said to Wells. They nodded to each other.

Soon the captain approached and the introductions began anew.

He said, "We seem to be missing a guest. We'll have to enjoy our time together without him."

I wondered who had stood up the captain. If the belligerent British chef was to be a late arrival, rougher seas could have been in my future.

The meals served at the usual dinners were quite good, but dinner at the captain's table seemed to take it up another notch. Which was not for the best—my stomach was unsettled from my earlier judging duties at the competition.

Plus, I hadn't taken it as easy at lunch as I should have.

More and more delectable courses kept on coming. When it was finally time for dessert, I just couldn't.

"No dessert for you, Mr. Murphy?" the captain asked. "Perhaps I can offer an alternative."

He whispered to the wine steward who soon returned with a special bottle of liquor and small glasses for each of us.

I read aloud the label on the bottle set down in front of the captain. "Navy Strength Rum. I don't think I've come across that before."

The captain said, "I don't bring this out for just anyone, Mr. Murphy, but you seem like a gentleman of great taste."

I was afraid my rented tuxedo had sent the man careening off in the wrong direction. But I didn't correct his course.

The wine steward poured a small amount of the brown liquid into each of our glasses. It seemed like a stingy amount to me, but maybe it was a very rare and expensive spirit. We toasted and I took a sip.

Yowser that was strong!

The captain noticed us choking and said, "You'll want to go easy on it. It's 114 proof. But it is tasty." He took a small sip.

It has a taste?

I soon regained enough control over my lips to speak. "Why is it called Navy Strength?"

"The story goes," the captain began, "that sailors in the Royal Navy regularly consumed rum but had a difficult time determining the actual alcohol content in what they procured."

Wells interrupted, as he got up to leave. "It has enough alcohol that if you combine it with gunpowder, the mixture will still ignite."

"Yes, that is the history," the captain concluded. He thanked us all for joining him for dinner and told us that he must return to his duties.

I zoned out a bit as Kimber and my mother chatted at the table until my stomach started to rebel from the day's sustenance and possibly the aperitif. I quickly excused myself.

Chapter Seventeen

My belly was not happy with my overindulgence in both good and not-so-good food that day, not to mention the captain's rum. But I wanted another shot at getting into that casino. *Surely it had to be open.*

And it was. I roamed the somewhat darkened room looking over glowing slot machines and green-felted gaming tables.

Which would have the honor of being the first to steal my dough?

I plopped onto an empty stool at a blackjack table and watched the current hand play out. It looked familiar enough.

I was finally going to get the chance to lose some money to the house—or the houseboat, in this case. As I made the ill-fated move to retrieve my keycard from my pocket for the buy-in, an ear-splitting tone came over the loudspeakers in the ceiling.

The klaxon was followed by a voice imploring, "Man overboard!" The tone and phrase repeated over and over and I shoved my fingers in my ears to try to protect my eardrums. I made for a door to the outside deck to escape the loud tone and the pleading, "Man overboard!" But it was no good—speakers blasted the alarm from everywhere.

Passengers and crew members were rushing in every direction. I tried to get out of the way on the wet deck as the ship turned and tried to stop. I was nearly knocked over the railing by a crewmate running with a life preserver ring.

I didn't know where everyone was heading—to the scene of the accident or somewhere away from the incessant noise. How could anyone help someone foundering in the black ocean ten stories below if they even survived the fall?

My stomach was roiling from the day's intake and all the panicked activity, and the cold wind made additional threats to my well-being. At least the earlier rain had ended.

I hurried to my cabin to check on my mother—she had said she was going there straight after dinner. I found her very obviously distressed. The loudspeaker in the cabin was also repeating the message but soon went quiet.

Was that good news?

In short order the loudspeaker in our room came to life again, but this time it asked everyone to gather at their lifeboat stations. It told us that it was not necessary to bring our life preservers. That was welcome news and I hoped there would be more of it to come. Maybe it had been a false alarm. Or maybe they had somehow recovered the unfortunate person.

We gathered in the small lobby of our lifeboat station and waited to hear what had happened. Lillianalisamarie, the cruise director, pointed at us one at a time and moved her lips as she counted to herself.

My mother tugged at my arm. "Where's Big Jim? Can you see him?"

I checked over the small group but Big Jim was nowhere in sight.

"No!" my mother cried. "Not Jim!"

"Mom, please don't jump to conclusions. He could be anywhere. I'm sure lots of people haven't made it to their gathering points, yet."

Lillianalisamarie stopped counting and made some notes on her clipboard.

I asked her, "Is it true that someone fell overboard? Can you tell us anything?"

"Not at this time. The captain will make an announcement when there is something to report. In the meantime," she raised her voice so that everyone in our small group could hear, "I need you all to let me know when you hear your name."

She called out each name on the list on her clipboard and there was a response to each callout, with one exception.

My mother muttered, "Oh, no."

We were all sent back to our cabins to wait for an announcement from the captain. I peeked outside on the way back and thought the ship still looked stationary, floodlights pointed at the water far below. I wondered how long they would search and how often they found someone alive after they fell from the deck.

Back at the cabin, I called in an order for a drink to soothe my mother and tried to calm her the best I could. "There are thousands on this ship. The odds that it was Big Jim are slim."

"It was him," she said.

"You can't know that." But somehow I felt she was right.

The next announcement came two hours later—I had drifted off to sleep but my mother woke me.

The captain sounded tired. "I am sorry to say that one of our passengers has fallen overboard and has been lost. Unfortunately, we haven't been able to recover them from the heavy seas. We will be underway again shortly. Anyone who is having difficulty coping is encouraged to see the Chaplain or a medical officer. If you think you might have information about the incident, please let a crew member know."

The statement was short and not very informative. We did learn it was a passenger and not a crew member. Beyond that, the announcement was carefully phrased to not even indicate if it was a man or a woman.

"Mom, would you like to talk to someone about it?"

"No, son. I'll be fine. I just wish they would tell us who it was. They should know by now."

I agreed. But I supposed the next of kin should be contacted first.

Chapter Eighteen

The following day I had expected to find a morose tone about the ship, but everything had already returned to normal. The weather had improved, bright sunlight invading the windows. I could hear the clang of the casino's slot machines, taunting me, and chatting and laughing guests were everywhere.

It was still too early to go to the studio and I thought about getting something to eat. My stomach recalled yesterday's overwhelmed state, suggesting it might be a good day to not break the night's fast.

Monica texted, calling a production meeting with all the cast and crew. I showed up right away but she wouldn't tell me what was going on. Soon everyone else had turned up with one telling exception.

The producer sighed. "It is with a heavy heart that I must tell you all that Big Jim James was the person who went overboard last night."

There was a gasp from the crowd.

My mother had been right.

But had it been an accident, perhaps aided by a bit too much of his favorite Tennessee whiskey? Jim's center of gravity might conflict with that conclusion. Or had he jumped? Big Jim seemed fine the last time I saw him. But you can never tell what bedevils a person on the inside. Certainly, the competition hadn't been too much for him. Even Cole was surviving it, if just barely. My previous experiences suggested something more sinister.

I couldn't hold my tongue. "Do they know what happened?"

"Please let me get through this, Murph." Her gaze swept her team. "The production is shut down for good. I will speak with each of you as to what happens next."

Wells jumped up. "I was winning. This isn't fair."

Monica retorted, "You know it wouldn't be right to continue with Big Jim dead. The decision is final."

Wells stomped out of the room. Chefs can be a bit high-strung. I would have to catch up with him later. Pointing out to him that he actually wasn't winning could help. Or maybe not.

I seized the moment, "Monica, can we talk privately?"

We stepped off to a corner of the studio. She was quiet and her eyes wet. I couldn't tell if she was mourning the loss of Big Jim or her production.

I asked, "Did they tell you anything else?"

"Nothing other than he was lost at sea, Murph. All I know for sure is that the show is over."

The nosy detective in me needed more.

Monica's phone chimed. I moved away to give her privacy, dragging my feet.

She took a quick look at the message. "Murph, wait. The captain has asked me to review some footage from last night's unfortunate accident. If you want to know more, you may tag along. Kimber told me you're quite the sleuth, for a food blogger."

We found our way to the ship's security room and knocked. The door opened and we were greeted by the captain and another officer.

"Miss Hastings, thank you for coming," the captain said. "And I see you brought a guest. Welcome, Mr. Murphy."

Our dinner must have been memorable.

"I thought Murph might be helpful as he's had considerable experience with these kinds of investigations," Monica offered.

"He could be. But I must insist that nothing you see here leave this room," the captain replied.

How ominous.

"Wilkins, would you play back the video?"

The officer clicked on a keyboard in front of a large screen. "We have cameras capturing important areas of the ship, but we didn't have a good angle to see what transpired last night."

The image on the screen was mostly dark until we saw someone walk into the shot.

Monica spoke up, "That sure looks like Big Jim."

I agreed. He was hard to miss.

The captain said, "Please keep watching."

After a moment, another man entered the shot and approached Big Jim. It was very dark and I couldn't tell who it was. "Can you up the brightness?" I asked the officer.

"I'm sorry, sir. This is the best I can do."

"Is there any sound?" If I couldn't see anything, identifying a voice could help.

"Recording sound is not allowed," Wilkins replied.

We watched as the two men in the video argued. It looked as if Big Jim started laughing. Then the other man punched him in the face and Big Jim fell out of camera view. The other man turned and walked off.

"Is there anything more?" I asked.

"No. That's it," the captain said. "Do either of you know who the other man is?"

"It's so dark, I don't think I can tell," Monica said.

"Can you play it again?" I asked.

I watched the replay twice more. "I think it's Chef Ken Gemani. I recognize his pickle-faced expression."

"Are you sure, Mr. Murphy?" the captain asked.

"I am not. But I can talk to him if you like."

"We will do that ourselves. And I would like to see footage from your show so that I can see this 'pickle-faced expression' for myself, or any other shots that you think might be relevant, Miss Hastings."

"Of course," Monica said.

We were expelled and I debated how to tell my mother the hard truth. She was already sure it was Big Jim so it wouldn't be a complete shock, but the confirmation of his fate might not be so easy to take.

Chapter Nineteen

My mother was stoic as I told her that the victim was indeed the man she had been spending her time with. Once I was sure she would be okay, or at least safe in our cabin, I started my probe in earnest.

I took metal stairs down to the crew decks in search of the brig. Rumor was Ken had already been detained and I wanted to talk to the prisoner in person. I passed the small morgue along the way—another reminder that death indeed does not take a vacation.

I rapped on the cell door that was adorned simply by a whiteboard with the prisoner's name and opened the conversation hole. "Ken? It's Murph Murphy. Mind if we have a chat?"

He seemed in good spirits, considering. "I know you. You're one of the judges for the cookoff. How is it going?"

"Given that one of the semi-finalists is dead and another is in jail, they've canceled the competition."

"That seems reasonable. So now you can tell me what you really thought of my sardine-nest Brussels sprout. I know you were just being kind in your critique."

"Was I kind?" I responded. "If you're asking if they gave me nightmares, let's say they were unforgettable."

"There you go being nice, again. Speaking of that, it's great to see a friendly face. I only get visits from people who keep asking me questions about last night."

"Well..."

"It's okay, Mr. Murphy. What can I do for you?" His pickle face was sincere.

"First off, it's Murph. Would you please talk me through last night? I've seen some video but I would like to hear from you."

"There's a video? Then they know I didn't do it!"

"Unfortunately, the camera didn't have a clear view. Tell me what happened."

"I didn't kill Big Jim is what happened! I was mad, that's for sure, but I would never kill anybody."

"Why did you have a meeting with him that evening?" I kept my cool, hoping Ken would follow suit.

"I didn't. I went out on the deck after dinner and saw him standing around like he was waiting for somebody."

"Was there anyone else around?"

"It was dark and I didn't see anybody else. I was tired and maybe a little buzzed so I thought it was a good time to have it out with him."

"Because he was ahead on the show?"

"No. I don't care about that. He's a great chef. His bacon brittle was nothing short of ethereal." The Canadian chef's expression echoed mine when I tried that same dish.

"Then what was your beef with him?"

"Um, it was business."

That didn't clarify anything. "I can't help you if you're not straight with me."

"I didn't kill him."

"But you did hit him."

"I did. He goaded me into it. I punched him right in his smug face and he fell to the deck."

"Then what happened?"

"I walked away while he lay there cursing me out." Ken leaned closer to the door, though he didn't lower his voice. "He was plenty alive."

"And that's it? You didn't see or hear anything else?"

"Nope. I went to the bar and put him out of my mind. I thought nothing more of it until I was hauled to the captain's office."

"Care to elaborate more on the 'business' you mentioned?" I needed something, anything.

"It was between me and him and now he's dead. So, no." He went to the back of his cell and sat down on the bed.

It seemed like I was to get no further clarity on what had happened. Maybe he did it. But it didn't feel right to me. His version of the story matched what I saw on the video. He slugged Big Jim turned and walked off. If he had seen Big Jim go over the side, I was sure he would have reacted.

"Thank you for talking to me," I said. "If you think of anything else, please let me know."

I closed the conversation hole and leaned back against the wall. I couldn't say he didn't do it, but I couldn't say he did, either.

It seemed the captain had made up his mind, though, meaning there could still be a killer loose on board who no one was looking for. I couldn't let that stand.

Wilkins came by and shepherded me from the off-limits area.

Chapter Twenty

Since my usual confidant, Irma, was parked very far away, at the Denver airport, I wandered topside and forward to the kennels to see if my furry namesake had any thoughts on the murder. It was visiting hours so you could guess who was there.

"Hello, Kimber," I said.

"Hi, Murph! Did you bring a treat for Murphy?" She had the happy little dog on her lap.

"Aren't I treat enough?"

She tilted her head, mirroring her fuzzball. "Have you solved the murder yet? You don't really think it was Ken, do you?"

Word traveled fast. "I'm not sure. We spoke and he did have some kind of quarrel with the victim."

"What about?"

"He wouldn't tell me."

"I could go talk to him," she offered.

"Why would he talk to you?"

"You're talking to me and I'm not sure you even like me."

She made a good point. "How is Murphy enjoying his cruise?" I reached out and gave the pup a pat on his flank.

"He seems happy enough. They take good care of him and I brought his favorite dog food. I just wish he could stay in my cabin. We've hardly ever been separated."

"Well, then, I'll leave you two to your snuggles. If you do happen to talk to Ken..."

"Don't worry. I'll let you know."

Talk of treats and food led me to notice that I was feeling a bit peckish.

Chapter Twenty-One

I loaded up a plate at the buffet. It was probably more rations than I needed right then, but what else was new? Most tables were full. I tried to find one that I could have to myself so that I could contemplate my next move. I walked further and further to the back and spotted a free table in an area that seemed to be populated with chowing ship crew members. I could ask if I was allowed to sit there, or I could sit.

I wasn't alone long before someone leaned over the table. I guessed I wasn't supposed to be there after all. I looked up.

She was tall and slender and dressed to the nines, or even the tens.

"May I join you?" she asked.

I stumbled to my feet. "Of course—please sit!" I pulled out her chair and slid it back in before taking mine again. She set her tray down in front of her.

I thrust out my hand. "Miss deDay, I'm Murph Murphy. I loved your show with Miss Moor the other night. It's a real pleasure to meet you!"

She smiled and took my hand. "Thank you, Mr. Murphy, but we have already met."

I was sure I would have remembered.

How much had I been drinking this trip?

"How could I possibly forget meeting someone as stunning as..." I looked past the heavy, purple eye-shadow, into pistachio-green eyes. "Arthur?"

"Yes, Mr. Murphy. It is I. I'm glad you enjoyed our show. Whatever happened with that runaway dog? Did you find out if he was the one you thought?"

"Please, call me Murph. Yes, it was actually Murphy, and his master is indeed on board."

She looked me up and down. "I can't tell if you're pleased or not. It must be some coincidence that Ms. Wilson is on the same cruise as you."

"It's never a coincidence when Kimber enters my orbit. It turns out that she's the one that got me the gig as a judge for Chefs at Sea. But enough about her. Why are you all dressed up today as your alter ego? Do you have another performance?"

"I just came from teaching a class on theater. I'm sure you would have enjoyed it, being a video star yourself." She fluttered her long eyelashes at me.

"I don't think my vlogs demonstrate your kind of star power. I am sorry I missed out on some professional training. Will there be another chance to see you?"

"I have one more show coming up in the theater on the last night of the cruise."

"I won't miss it."

Chapter Twenty-Two

I had been wanting to try the afternoon tea service, but my mother had bailed on me. I couldn't blame her—she was still mourning Big Jim. Most of the events on the ship were open to singles and afternoon tea was no exception. But, luckily enough, I crossed paths with Wells on my way to the dining room and he agreed to join me.

He filled me in on the highlights. "The afternoon tea offered on the QA2 is adequate, but it pales in comparison to the finer high teas around London. You will make time for at least one of those once we arrive in the UK, won't you? I can make some recommendations."

"We'll only be in town for a day before I have to fly home. I had to sandwich the cruise in between some other commitments. I can try to fit in a high tea, but it all depends on how my mother is doing."

"Oh, is she feeling ill?"

"It's nothing time won't heal."

A hostess seated us in the remaining two chairs at one of the big round tables in the dining room. The other guests at the table were already sipping from fancy teacups while scones and finger sandwiches decorated fine china plates in front of them.

A server set down our tea cups and offered to pour from a silver teapot. A selection of finger sandwiches was brought around next, followed by warm scones with clotted cream and strawberry jam. I could make a meal of the many selections but was careful not to repeat my bellyaching of the previous night. I took pictures and made a few notes. I sat back and took a long sip of my tea. Most of the other guests had left our table by then.

I said, "So, tell me about Big Jim, Wells."

"What?"

"You knew him personally, right? I only know what I have seen of him on TV."

"Oh, yes, I could count him among my friends." Wells smiled.

"Did he have any enemies?"

"Doesn't everyone? I mean outwardly he was an affable guy, but he had an empire to build and you can't do that without creating a few hard feelings."

I could finally be getting somewhere. "Were any of those ill feelings held by someone on the show?"

"Was there anyone on the show who hadn't been affected by Big Jim is the better question. Take Avery for example. She didn't like him even a little. There were rumors about some kind of relationship gone bad during another show, but I wasn't around for that one."

"I get the feeling that there are very few people Avery likes. She doesn't think my chosen profession is worthy. Who else had secrets?"

"Everyone has their secrets. Big Jim knew most everybody's. It...helped...him with his business dealings, let's say."

"Are you implying blackmail?" I sat up straight in my seat, almost spilling my tea.

"Jim would never be so gauche. He knew secrets weren't meant to be kept—they were meant to be shared, judiciously, under the right circumstances, with the right parties, even if they weren't entirely factual." Wells stared into his cup as he swirled his tea, then set it down, looking at me. "If you know what I mean."

I wasn't sure that I did.

Perhaps a different line of questioning would get me a clue. "Someone would have to be in fairly good shape to boost Big Jim over that railing."

"I've seen Ken in the gym on the ship and he knows his way around a weight rack. I have no doubt he could have done it."

"There's a gym on board?"

"I can see you might not know that." Wells glanced towards my ample midriff.

"But why would Ken do it? He told me he confronted Big Jim about 'business,' but he wouldn't tell me more."

"I'm not surprised that he wouldn't tell you why he killed Big Jim. I don't know the specifics, but Jim was an 'investor' in Ken's latest restaurant." He made quotes in the air.

"An investor?"

"Big Jim had his hands in the pockets of half the chefs on that stage. He would sign on as a silent partner but he didn't know the meaning of the words. I'm sure there are a lot of chefs breathing a sigh of relief right now."

"Wouldn't they still have to pay him back? Or rather pay his company or estate?"

Wells laughed. "Get real, Murph! It was all under the table—there was no paperwork. Nobody has to pay back anything."

"That makes it sound like anyone he invested in would have a motive to kill him. Why do you think it was Ken who did it?"

He picked up his teacup again. "I heard there is some kind of evidence against him. Something about them arguing before Jim took a dive."

"Yeah, there's a video."

Wells set his teacup onto its plate with a clatter. "A video?"

"It doesn't show much. It was dark and didn't have a good angle. But you could see enough to tell that Ken was not happy with Big Jim."

"Then it sounds like it's a wrap. I think I've had enough tea." He pushed himself away from the table.

"Please don't tell anyone I told you about the video," I beseeched.

Chapter Twenty-Three

The magician I'd seen on stage in Roo deDay's show was doing a demo in one of the lounges. I could use a little magic to help solve this case. Or maybe it would give me a diversion to get the case off my mind for a short time, even though time was running out. It wouldn't be that long till we docked in England and any suspects would be in the wind.

Marvelous Mac performed a few of the tricks I had seen in his show. He also did some close-up sleight of hand that was supernatural, with cards disappearing and reappearing in impossible places. I couldn't figure out how he did any of it, and that wasn't helping my confidence in solving my own predicament.

He then opened up the floor for questions. A man up front had the nerve to ask the big one, "How does the 1-2-3 trick work?"

"Did everyone see that trick during my show?" Mac asked the small crowd.

There were a few nods.

"For those who didn't, shall we try one here?"

There was a smattering of applause indicating approval.

"How about this gentleman—would you like to help with the trick?"

He was looking in my direction. I looked behind me but didn't see the gentleman he was referring to.

"Yes, you sir. What's your name?"

"Murph."

"Are you familiar with the game?"

I nodded.

"A man of few words. That should be very entertaining for the audience."

The audience laughed and my face felt hot.

"OK, Murph. I think I'm reading you. Let's start with 1 car."

"That would be Irma," I offered.

"2 coworkers."

I thought a moment—I usually worked alone. "The other two judges on the show."

"3..." He paused

I jumped in, "Don't say ex-wives."

That got a laugh.

"I was going to say yesterday's desserts, but I think 3 is undercounting."

That got a bigger laugh.

"I'm a food critic. Dessert is in my job description."

"Thank you, Murph. That should give everyone an idea of how the game works. While I can't reveal the secrets of any specific trick, I would like to remind you that I've been on this cruise for as long as the rest of you. I don't magically appear right before my show, though that would be convenient."

The guy down front who had asked the 1-2-3 question laughed hard.

Mac continued, "People make a lot of small talk right out in the open, sometimes speaking of very personal things, and not considering who else might be listening."

The questioner didn't look satisfied, but I thought I got it. Surreptitious eavesdropping combined with a memory less like a colander than mine was the better portion of that trick.

I stuck around until everyone else, other than Mac, had left. I got close, but not too close and I didn't offer my hand—I liked my watch.

And my wallet. And my phone. And my room keycard.

"Can I ask you a question, Mac?"

"Not about the 1-2-3 I did for you, I hope? You know I can't reveal my secrets."

"No, you gave us a good idea about how that works. What I would like to ask you about are other people's secrets."

"How so?"

"As you mentioned, you've been hanging around this ship, taking it all in, shall we say. I'm looking into the murder of Big Jim James, the man who went overboard, and wondered if you happened to hear anything that might point to a motive?"

He stuffed a deck of cards into his coat jacket. "I was in the audience for Chefs at Sea a couple of times."

"I was pretty focused on my tasting duties. Did you notice any conflict with anyone on the show?"

"It mostly went very smoothly. However, there was an argument between Mr. James and someone else after a show."

I got excited. "Do you know who he was arguing with?"

"A skinny kid. I've seen him around collecting autographs."

I walked away with a few new ideas for my case. I glanced at my wrist—where was my watch?

Nuts!

Oh yeah, it was safe at home—I hadn't brought it on the trip.

Chapter Twenty-Four

I had a new suspect in that autograph hound whom Mac told me Jim had argued with. There were also other fans on the ship, and maybe even a stalker or two. Plus, it seemed like everybody on Chefs at Sea had a motive to see Big Jim disappear. None of this was very helpful in narrowing down my suspect list.

I had to start somewhere, and the producer, Monica was central to the show. She might be able to tell me something about my other suspects and I could try to rule her out at the same time. I sent her a message and she suggested meeting at the bar. When I got there I could see she was already halfway through her second highball.

"Hi, Murph. Grab a stool. I don't need to be drinking alone this early in the day."

"Hi, Monica. What are you celebrating?" I asked, trying to lighten the mood.

"The end of my career. This show was my baby. I cost the studio more money than I could make in a lifetime. I'm washed up."

"It's not your fault, is it?" Might as well take the direct approach.

"I was the one who convinced the studio that a cooking show on a cruise ship would be a good idea. Then I convinced the sponsors, the biggest of which is this cruise company, that it would pay off. But now it won't. We can't use any of it. There will be lawsuits and blackballing. I should probably join Big Jim."

"You can't be serious," I hoped.

"No, I'm not going to jump. But I am considering moving to Scotland after we land. Nobody knows me there."

"Before you go into hiding, can you tell me what you know about the people on the show? Did you pick them all yourself?"

"For the most part. The studio wanted to use the host, Declan Beige, and Avery. The rest were based on availability. Usually, these kinds of shows shoot in a few days. Getting everyone together for over a week was tough. But I pulled it off. And look what it got me." She dove back into her glass.

"I can't imagine you would choose Cole as a judge."

"I owed his agent a favor. She may have misrepresented Cole's qualifications a little. There wasn't time to interview him before we left. I appreciate you taking him under your wing."

"I did what I could for him, but I don't think he'll ever grow to relish food like me. Did you know that Avery and Big Jim had a previous relationship?"

"If I had to pick people based on who had been with who, or who hated who, I would have never been able to cast it. I figured the blind judging would lessen the chance of payback. Did you notice something off?" She looked concerned, even though it was all going into the bin.

"No, it seemed reasonably fair to me. But what do I know? I haven't done this before any more than Cole. Were there any problems you saw?"

"I was surprised at how well it was going—until Ken dispatched Big Jim."

"Why are you so sure it was Ken?"

Monica concentrated on twisting a cherry stem between her fingers. "Kimber said you were an intrepid investigator."

"I want to make sure they have the right guy. Apparently, many others had reason to see Big Jim leave the ship before we got to port."

"I don't know it was Ken. But it makes no difference. I'm washed up no matter who did it. Will you visit me in Scotland?" She had such a sad look.

"The next time I get that way I'll buy you a haggis."

Chapter Twenty-Five

One by one, with Monica's help, I ran down and interviewed the other contestants on the show. Of the chefs, most had alibis, even the British chef, Miles Stonegate. Only the French chef had no one who could confirm his whereabouts when Big Jim went over. I still needed to interview the other judges and the show's host.

I found Avery at afternoon tea. I took the empty seat next to her. "Hi, Avery. Got a minute?"

"Hello, Mr. Murphy. As far as I know, there are no more judging duties so we no longer need to interact."

I think I was dismissed—that wouldn't do. "I wanted to tell you what a pleasure it was to work with you. I learned so much and I should be better prepared the next time I'm offered a chance to judge."

She seemed to soften slightly. "Thank you, Mr. Murphy." But only ever so slightly. "I certainly hope you will be better prepared if by chance anyone ever foolishly calls upon you again."

Ouch.

"I also wanted to offer my condolences to you over Big Jim."

"Why would you want to do that?"

"I understand you had had a past relationship with him."

"And what if I did? That was the distant past. I harbored no more feelings for him than I did for that overcooked horse he served us."

That sure sounded like feelings. There was still some smoke there if not fire.

"When did you see him last?"

"Same as you—at the judging."

I wanted to ask, "And before that, and before that," but I knew she had the propensity to storm off.

"And where were you when Big Jim met his watery fate?"

"I was in my suite."

"Alone?"

"My personal life is just that." She stormed off.

A steward offered me tea to soothe my injured feelings.

I sipped the charity and pondered how to find the autograph hound who had argued with Big Jim. I had to find one person in almost 4000, and I didn't know his name. I needed some bait and had an idea. I still wanted to talk to Cole to see if he had an alibi for that night. With Big Jim gone and the show canceled, Cole had managed to get off the hook and not have to eat another chef's special.

Was that enough for a motive?

I banged on the door of Cole's cabin—loudly, and several times. He propped it open with his foot, his head down in his phone. I squeezed past him, sat in a chair, and waited. He finished his level and paused the game, finally noticing who had come into his cabin.

"Mr. Murphy. We don't have to eat anything else, do we?"

"Not for the show, but I assume you'll still need to eat again before the cruise is over. Do you mind if I ask you where you were when Big Jim went overboard?"

"You mean, did I have an alibi?"

"I'm just being thorough and asking everyone. I hope you don't mind." I didn't expect he would make like Avery and storm out, as we were in his stateroom.

Cole set his phone on the desk. "I was in the penthouse with Emily, at the time. Her husband Edgar had been taken to the hospital and she needed consoling. I offered her a brandy, not realizing it was her husband's favorite, causing her to break down. I'm sure she'll corroborate."

What? "Who are Emily and Edgar?"

"Those were lines from my last movie. I guess you didn't see it. I was in the bar. Someone probably saw me there."

I had not seen it. "How did your agent take the news that the show was shut?"

"She was not happy that I wouldn't be getting the chance to improve my image."

"I had an idea about that. What if you hold a meet and greet with your fans onboard? I'm sure we could get the cruise director to arrange it for us. If you're extra nice to your fans and they come away happy, your agent might cut you some slack."

"There won't be any food, will there?"

"None that you have to eat. We'll set up a half-hour session to sign autographs and chat in one of the lounges. You can be on your best behavior for half an hour, right?"

"I'll just smile and read my lines." He gave me a toothy grin.

This could work. It should draw out my autograph hound and give me a chance to interview them. However, I could use an assistant and my mother was still out of service. I checked my phone—it was still visiting hours at the kennel.

Chapter Twenty-Six

My next interview subject filled me with elation and anxiety. Monica had arranged for me to meet with Declan Beige—*Declan Beige!* He was all alone in the closed French restaurant, looking for all the world like he owned the place, which, maybe he did.

He greeted me as I entered. "Murph Murphy— competition judge and food blogger extraordinaire. Come, have a seat."

I could feel my face go the color of a beet while I clumsily yanked out a chair at his table. "Thank you for agreeing to meet with me, Mr. Beige."

"We're all friends here—call me Declan."

I looked around the empty room. *All?*

He didn't mince words. "I expect you're here to find out if I'm the murderer."

"No…umm…yes…I—"

"I certainly hope you are or you wouldn't be doing your diligence." He grinned like a Cheshire.

"You know what I do?"

Was I pleased? Was I frightened?

"I do my research. I found your blog very entertaining—a high-style mix of food discovery and crime solving."

I supposed I was pleased. "Thank you. While I seek out my food content, the murders seem to find me on their own."

"And now you have another," he pointed out.

"Indeed, I do. But I'm sure you had nothing to do with it."

"How would you know that? I would be perfectly capable of tossing Big Jim to the sharks."

What was he saying?

He tented his fingers. "It's quite intriguing. I believe everyone on that show had equal opportunity to be victor or washout, victim or killer. I can see why you would be drawn to these mysteries."

I had to come out and ask, "Would you have a reason to be involved?"

"We're all involved, Murph. Without all the players, the play cannot go on. The question is fair, though—did I have a motive to kill Big Jim?"

I hoped not. Declan Beige was an idol to me. He was the person I would most like to be when I grew up.

He dropped his hands to his lap. "I was not Jim James' biggest fan. I'm sure you've learned quite a bit about him in your interrogations and you know he was not who he portrayed."

I nodded, prompting him to continue.

"But he was not my problem to solve. As far as I could tell, he didn't rise to the level of being truly evil. He was more opportunist, and very good at creating those opportunities for himself."

So, if he had been truly evil? This man was not what I had expected.

I timidly asked, "Do you have an alibi? It's okay if you don't."

"I spent the moments before the sirens with the stage magician, Mac. We traded a few secrets—card tricks before you get too excited."

Servers were starting to mill about the restaurant so I needed to wrap this up. There was so much more I had wanted to talk to him about, but much as Big Jim wasn't who he seemed, I was afraid that if I stayed, I might find the same about Declan Beige.

Chapter Twenty-Seven

Another note on my cabin door—I couldn't imagine the captain wanted me back for dinner. He did not. The note was made up of cuttings from what appeared to be the daily program of shipboard activities, to create a special message just for me, "Stop or your mother is next."

Short though certainly not sweet. I must have been getting close—but I didn't know to what. What I did know was that I had put my mother in harm's way. I needed to get the killer in handcuffs as soon as possible.

I still had a long list of suspects and maybe the note could help narrow the list a bit. Its author had to know I was traveling with my mother—not a secret but probably not something just anyone would know.

I had to find my mother right away and make her aware that I put a target on her back. I didn't have to search far—she was inside our cabin, resting in her bed.

I said quietly, "Mom, are you awake?"

"Who's asking? Are you that nice cabin boy with my wine?"

At least she still had her sense of humor.

She propped herself up in bed and I handed her the note. "I found this on the door. I don't want to worry you, but you should know."

I studied her face as she read the threat. I couldn't tell if it upset her or scared her, or discern any emotion at all. I guessed she was still numb.

She said, "I'm not worried, son. This makes it seem like Ken didn't do it if he's still locked up."

Smart woman. "I agree. Is there anything you need?"

"I'm fine, just a bit tired. I'll be having dinner in my room tonight."

"That sounds like it's for the best. Are you okay to talk about Big Jim with me?"

"I think so."

"You spent a good deal of time with him. Did he mention any reason why anyone would want to hurt him?"

"No, I can't imagine why anyone would want to. He was such a sweetheart."

I knew differently, but I didn't feel the need to correct her. "Did he ever talk about anyone in the show?"

"Oh, he told lots of funny stories about some of them. He was never at a lack of a tall tale to tell. He probably embellished them for added fun. But he told so many, I'm not sure I can remember them well enough to tell you who they were about."

"If you do think of anything that stands out, let me know. In the meantime, don't let anyone in, other than your favorite room steward, of course."

I went immediately to find the captain and show him the note. I knocked on the glass door of the ship's bridge and the crewman that answered said he would send the captain out to see me.

"Mr. Murphy," the captain said, "how can I help you?"

I held out the note. "I found this on my cabin door. It looks like a threat."

"Let's have a look." He took the paper from me and glanced at it. "We get pranks like this all the time. I'm sure it's nothing to worry about." He handed it back to me.

"If Ken Gemani is still in the brig, he couldn't have put the note on my door," I proffered.

"Mr. Gemani will stay locked away until we reach England. I assure you that you and your mother are quite safe."

I didn't feel assured at all. Even if the note wasn't enough to spring Ken, it should at least have been cause to continue the inquiry into Big Jim's death. I started to wonder if the captain had a lobster in this roll.

Chapter Twenty-Eight

Kimber had agreed to help me with my plan and I met her and Cole at the lounge a few minutes before the autograph session I had arranged was scheduled to begin. Cole was dressed nicer than he had been for the show and his ubiquitous phone was nowhere to be seen.

"Just smile and be friendly," I said to him.

He offered me a friendly smile.

A small crowd had started forming at the roped-off entrance to the lounge. I looked for my conquest but didn't see anyone who fit the description.

At the appointed hour, Kimber removed the rope and people surrounded Cole. He was quite at ease as he posed for pictures and signed anything and everything presented to him, including some bare flesh. His short stack of headshots soon disappeared and the crowd thinned.

I had yet to see the one person I had arranged this for. Maybe he hadn't seen the advertising.

Time was up. Cole thanked me for organizing this—his agent would be pleased—and we exited the lounge. A young guy in a ballcap leaning against the far wall came forward and intercepted Cole as we left.

Bingo.

Apparently, the hound did not like crowds and wanted Cole to himself.

"I hope I'm not too late to get an autograph," the guy cooed.

Cole was still amenable and said, "No problem. But I'm afraid I'm out of headshots."

"That's okay. I brought these for you to sign."

The hound produced several sheets of fine white paper along with a permanent marker. It looked like somebody had a good business plan.

As Cole amiably signed each of the pages, I nudged Kimber with my elbow. She put her hand out to the hound, "I'm Kimber. What's your name?"

This seemed to take him aback. His gaze darted around the corridor. "Um, Chase."

Kimber pulled her unwelcomed hand back.

Chase? Something wasn't right. He dashed off as soon as Cole signed the last page. I looked around as the hound had done and found a placard labeling one of the corridor's columns—Pipe Chase.

Chapter Twenty-Nine

Kimber and I followed "Chase" back to his cabin, keeping our distance so our quarry wouldn't get spooked. A cabin number might help get me a real name.

"What's the plan?" Kimber asked.

Plan, plan. I should probably have had one of those. "Maybe he wants my autograph?"

"I didn't mean your plan for fame—I meant a plan to find out what he knows."

"I know, I know."

As Kimber stood out of sight, I knocked on his door. A woman with long, blonde hair answered. For no particular reason I had assumed the hound would be alone, even though most cabins were doubles.

"Hi. Sorry to disturb you. I'm looking for your..." The longer I looked at her the more she looked like the hound. "...brother?"

"He's not here," she said as she tried to block my view.

I stuck my head in the best I could and saw the "not here" brother's cap on the bed. She glanced back at the bed and I took the opportunity to get a foot inside the stateroom.

Kimber and I had had the cabin door in sight since we saw "Chase" go in, and the inside stateroom had no other exit—he had to be in there. I took a quick look into the open bathroom, seeing only a smudged washcloth on the sink. She was alone in the room. I was perplexed until I looked down at what she was wearing—the same clothing as the hound.

"I'm a bit confused," I said. "I could have sworn you had a five o'clock shadow a few minutes ago."

She looked terrified and hurriedly pulled me inside, closing the cabin door behind me. "Please, you can't say anything. You can't tell anyone about me."

A stowaway? I didn't think that was possible with all the security to get on the ship.

"Then you'll have to tell me what's going on." At least I had some leverage. "What's your name? I'm pretty sure it's not Chase."

"It's Andrea Park." She sat down on the edge of the bed, looking for all the world like her life was over.

I didn't want to be hard on her, but I did want to find out if she knew anything about the murder or even was the murderer. "Why can't I tell anyone about you?"

"Because I'm supposed to be my twin."

That was unexpected, but unexpected is a twin trademark.

"This sounds like a story that you should start at the beginning." I pulled out the desk chair and sat down, facing her.

"My brother and I signed up for this cruise together with the idea that we could get autographs to sell later and help pay for the trip to London."

"So where is your brother?"

"He's still in New York." She picked up the hat off the bed and twisted it.

"Did he miss the boat?"

"No. I lost my passport on the way to New York and couldn't get a replacement before the ship left. He wouldn't go without me. He said I'm the one who can get the best autographs and he's the one who sells them online."

I finally got a clue. "So you dressed like him and used his passport to get onboard. Very tricky, and dangerous."

"That's why you can't tell anyone about me. You won't, will you?" she pleaded.

"That depends on what you can tell me about the death of Big Jim. I know you argued with him."

"He was the one chef who wouldn't give me an autograph. He wanted $200 for it. He wasn't very nice about it either."

Big Jim always gave the aura of being a sweet guy, but the more I learned about him the more the façade fell away. I was glad he didn't get his hooks into my mother.

"That could be motive for murder," I said.

"I swear I didn't kill him. You have to believe me. I stayed away from him after that."

I wanted to believe her, but if Big Jim had found out her secret, that was a much better motive than $200. But she still had other problems to face. "What's your plan once you get off the ship in England?"

"I'm supposed to send my brother's passport back to him so that he can fly over for the rest of our trip. He'll bring my replacement passport and we can both fly home together."

I had to crush that fantasy. "That's not going to work. Once you use his passport to enter England, he won't be able to reenter on it. He'd be caught by security at one end or the other, and then you'd be here without a passport and he could be in prison."

"We didn't think about that. What will I do?"

The pained look in her eyes made me want to do whatever I could to help this innocent child. I could see why she was the one who collected the autographs. "The safest thing would be to fly home right away on his passport and hope you don't get caught."

"But we saved for this trip for years. We already couldn't do the cruise together. Isn't there another way?" There were those eyes, again.

"Well," I couldn't believe I was saying this, "then he'll need to dress like you and fly to London on your passport. You can swap them back as soon as he gets here and have the trip you planned." That might have been the worst advice I had ever given.

She smiled. "We used to trade places all the time. With a wig and some makeup, that could work," she said, excitedly. "You won't tell anybody?"

"I won't." I wouldn't tell anybody in charge, but I couldn't leave Kimber out of the loop. "So, do you want my autograph while I'm here?"

"Oh. Of course. Are you somebody?"

"My mother seems to think so. I was one of the judges on the cooking show."

"That's right, you're the blogger. I guess somebody might want your autograph. And I did get the other judges, now that I have Cole's."

"Avery gave you her autograph?"

"Yeah, she was really nice."

Must not have been the same Avery I knew.

I signed an autograph page and left her to message her brother about the change of plans.

Kimber was still waiting down the hall, keeping guard. "Well?" she demanded.

"I don't think she did it."

"She?"

"Shush," I said. "We can't talk here. I'll fill you in later."

"How about at dinner? You once told me you always have to eat."

My mother wasn't up for dinner out that night. I didn't mind spending it alone with my suspect list or with whomever the dining room hostess matched me up with, but what could it hurt? "Okay. Dinner. Do you think we could get into the steak place? I forgot to make reservations earlier."

"I'll take care of it," she said. "Six?"

"Sure."

Kimber swept off down the long hallway, her brightly-colored bathing suit cover-up billowing behind her.

Chapter Thirty

At 6 p.m. sharp Kimber was waiting for me in the hallway outside of Jesters Steak House. She was dressed as nicely as she had been for the captain's dinner—I was not. I was starting to get the feeling that she thought this might be more than just dinner.

"Shall we?" she said as she took my arm and piloted me toward the hostess stand.

My feeling was a step closer to being confirmed. "We shall." My voice may have wavered a little.

The hostess led us to a small table against a window with a view of the waning day over the unending ocean. I made the effort to pull out Kimber's chair before plopping into my own.

Kimber looked over her menu and then closed it. "What are we having?"

"What do you mean?" She was a big girl and could order for herself. It wasn't like either of us had to pay the bill.

"I know you like to try out more than one dish for your blog. I'm sure I'll be happy with whatever you choose for me."

I set my menu down in front of me. I looked across the table and contemplated the person who may or may not be my nemesis. The golden light from the fading sunset on the horizon danced across her face. I had never really looked at her as a woman before.

"Kimber," I started, not exactly sure how to proceed. "You don't seem quite yourself lately. Is everything okay?" I didn't want to get too specific and end up embarrassing either of us.

"I'm sorry. I miss my Murphy so much. I think he misses me, too."

What?

"We haven't spent a night apart since I adopted him. And now it's been almost a week that he's been stuck in that kennel."

Oh—her Murphy. I had never, as I thought about it, seen her without him.

"He's been the only constant in my life—the one always there for me—since my divorce.

Murphy gives me purpose—a reason to get out of bed in the morning."

Kimber always seemed so strong and confident. I had never bothered to find out who she really was. Nemesis or not, it was time I treated her as the friend she had been to me.

"While I'm a poor substitute, I'll happily be your companion for the evening," I offered.

"I'm sorry. I didn't mean to dump that on you, Murph."

"It's okay—I'm glad to get to know you a little better. Now, what shall we have for dinner?" I picked up my menu and hid behind it while we both composed ourselves.

We spent far longer at Jesters than I had imagined we would. I was planning on taking one more shot at that accursed casino before lights out, but the entire evening had slipped effortlessly away from us. We had spent it comparing notes on our food, complete with photos, naturally, and laughing way too much. Two bottles of wine likely had something to do with it.

After the plates had been cleared, I quietly related what had happened with the autograph hound. Then Kimber patiently helped me go over my suspect list. We eliminated extraneous members of the ship's crew and the general public, including Lilliannalisamarie—she would probably have preferred tossing me over the side rather than Big Jim. And the captain certainly would have a better way of disposing of someone that wouldn't put a big dent in his sailing schedule.

The autograph hound still had me on the fence. If Jim had found out her secret, she would have a pretty good motive. But could she have coerced her weighty victim over the side?

For the time being, we chose to focus on people directly involved with the competition. That included all the chefs, even those that had alibis, the producer Monica, the other two judges, and even the show's host, Declan Beige.

"Do you think your hero had a good reason to do it?" Kimber asked.

"My hero?"

She stared me down.

"Fine," I relented. "I came away from my conversation with Declan believing that he was capable of pretty much anything, and might have already gotten away with far more than murder. But—"

"That would put him at the top of the list. You know you can't let your personal feelings cloud your judgment. It could be a deadly mistake."

"But," I reiterated, "he has an alibi I can easily check, and I will do so in the morning. And I can't see a motive that would force his hand to act before the competition was over. So, not the top of the list, but still on it for the moment."

"Monica, then," Kimber suggested.

"Jim's death was all downside for Monica, the best I can tell. It has probably cost her her career. She took on most of the risk for the production. She's safe."

"Safe?"

"Sorry, food competition jargon. She's off the list. Let's look at Cole next."

Kimber offered her thoughts. "I don't think he had anything to gain from the show being shut down. And he didn't know Big Jim outside the show, did he?"

"I don't think so. His biggest benefit from no more judging is never having to eat anything other than French fries for the rest of his life. But I agree it's a stretch for him to have done it. Avery on the other hand…"

"I've never understood why they have someone as hard to please as she is on these shows."

I took the last swig from my wine glass. "Drama. Conflict. However you want to look at it. That's what people tune in to see. Watching someone cook food can be fairly boring. Viewers showed up for the earliest TV shows like Julia Child's as much to see what trouble she would get into as how to cook a particular dish."

"So where does that put Avery?" Kimber asked.

"On the list."

"That leaves all the chefs to consider."

"Then let's consider them," I said. "I still believe Ken didn't do it. If he did, they already have him. Not on the list."

"Wells was with us at the captain's dinner that night," Kimber remembered.

She flagged down the server. I hoped she wasn't ordering another bottle of wine. I already needed a ride-share to get me back to my cabin. She requested the one dessert on the menu that we hadn't tried, a fruit trifle, and two spoons.

I was unlikely to wake up in time for breakfast anyway. "Wells said that half the competitors were in bed with Jim, but he didn't spell out who they were."

"Literally in bed?"

"Possibly, but in bed businesswise was what I meant."

"Any guesses who?"

"It's hard to tell. I can't eliminate the non-US chefs as it's a global business these days. I can say that Chef Miles Stonegate was more than a little menacing. He was very unhappy with my verdict for his dish, and being soundly beaten by Jim and voted off first is pretty embarrassing."

"You should go talk to him again."

"Did you not hear the 'menacing' part?" My plan was not to run into him for the rest of the cruise.

"What about the other chefs who were voted off?"

"I don't think that gives them as much motive as being first. While winning might give them a leg up—another award to add to their credentials—losses fall by the wayside quickly. Direct past dealings with Big Jim seem to offer the best motive."

We weighed the pros and cons of the rest of the contenders as we dipped our spoons into the trifle. Many still needed their alibis verified. And I also wondered if we had taken the wrong people off the list.

Our final dessert challenge met and recorded, I walked Kimber, arm in arm, back to her cabin.

Chapter Thirty-One

It was the penultimate day of the cruise. The next morning, we would awaken docked in Southampton. This would be my last chance to find a way to flush out the killer. If I didn't, Ken would be put in chains as soon as he left the ship, and I was now positive that he didn't do it.

I had had a fitful night—too much wine could sometimes do that to me—thinking about Kimber, along with who else in my life I might not be considering in the proper light. And during the tossing and turning I realized what, or rather who, had been staring me in the face.

I formulated a plan. I needed to get a message to Arthur, and then I needed to send one to Kimber. I wanted to make sure she knew I had enjoyed our time out last night.

My mother was almost back to her old self. I took her to a late breakfast.

She began the conversation like any concerned parent. "Did you go broke at the casino last night?"

"No, I never made it. And I never will. That place is cursed."

"Then, where were you all night?"

"It wasn't all night," I contested. "I was having dinner with a friend."

"And how has Wells been doing, since Chefs at Sea was canceled?"

"I wasn't with Wells."

"Who, then?"

I felt like one of my suspects. "Mother, it was Kimber, okay?"

"Why are you being so defensive? I was only asking."

I always seemed to fall back into this kind of relationship with my mother. I think she's prying and wanting to tell me how to live my life. But I knew she wasn't. I knew I was being too sensitive, like some little kid. It was time I grew up and at least acted as if we were both adults.

"I'm sorry, Mom. Kimber and I went out to dinner at Jesters."

"That place is very nice and cozy. Big Jim took me there, once." A distant look entered her eyes and a brief smile flickered across her lips.

"It was very nice. Even though I know it's the same food as the rest of the restaurants onboard, it tasted so much better in those surroundings."

"And with that company?" my mother gently prodded.

"Kimber and I are just friends."

"That sounds like an upgrade from the way you usually talk about her."

"Maybe she's not the person I thought she was. Or maybe I never thought at all."

Chapter Thirty-Two

It was the final evening show of the cruise. As I entered the theater, I noticed Cole sitting next to Chef Miles—the man had served him probably his favorite meal of the cookoff, a bland sandwich. Mac the magician sat a few seats down from them.

Wells and I had front-row seats—close enough to see the green of Roo deDay's eyes one last time. She had come on stage to great applause.

"Thank you all for attending our closing performance." She took a low bow. "It has been our pleasure to have entertained you this past week on the resplendent Queen Alex 2. Before my partner, Misti Moor, joins me onstage, I would like to invite up a couple of passengers as representatives of Chefs at Sea, the ill-fated cooking competition we had onboard." She pointed to myself and Wells.

As we were slow to cooperate, she added, "Let's move it, boys—don't make me come down there to get you—you know I will."

The audience tittered.

Wells and I made our way up the stairs. She positioned us on either side of her, holding our hands. I squinted in the bright light, surveying what I could see of the audience. Declan Beige, Monica, and Avery sat together, and the captain was in his special box, along with the cruise director, Lillianalisamarie.

Miss deDay said, "Would you each please introduce yourselves to our audience?" She turned my way first.

"I'm Murph Murphy, one of the judges of Chefs at Sea." No applause. *It was okay. Really.*

Wells jumped in, obviously loving the spotlight. "And I'm Welland Goode, the top competitor of the entire show." The man did not hold back.

There was a smattering of applause. Clearly the audience was looking for a better time than this.

Miss deDay's tone became somber, "I usually don't like to start my show on a heavy note, but I'm sure you all remember there was a tragedy as one of the cooking show competitors was lost overboard."

There was murmuring from the crowd.

"But I have amazing news," her voice rising. "A fishing boat was able to recover Big Jim James the next morning after we had sailed on. That boat has finally caught up with us and delivered a very special guest. Please help me welcome back Big Jim James!"

The audience gasped. Wells and I looked toward the back curtain of the stage where Roo had motioned and I saw a shadow of a stout person in a chef's hat.

Wells started tugging at Roo deDay's hand. She held tight to him, and to me—I was her anchor.

"Unhand me, woman," Wells proclaimed. He struggled but she held fast.

I tried to settle him down. "What's wrong, Wells? This is a pretty exciting development."

"You know very well what's wrong." He wrestled to free himself again as he looked toward the back curtain.

"What do you mean?" I asked, feigning ignorance.

Wells stopped struggling, if only for the moment. "It's Jim's word against mine, and he's a liar. It's vegan—it's all vegan," he shouted at the shadow.

"Perhaps you should tell us what happened that night before he comes on stage," I offered.

The room got quiet.

"I just happened to be on deck, walking off a big dinner. I saw Ken punch Big Jim and run off. I helped Jim up and made sure he was okay. I thought he was fine when I left him, but that punch must have rattled his brain. If he fell or even jumped over the side after that, it isn't on me."

I could see the wheels turning behind Wells' eyes as he struggled to come up with a convincing tale—a fish tale at that.

He kept paddling, "Or Ken came back to finish the job—and frame me for the murder."

"Why would Ken want to frame you?" I asked.

"He...I..." Wells seemed out of excuses.

I pushed a little harder. "It wasn't like you helped Jim up and then over the railing, was it? Let's get Big Jim out here and see what he has to say."

"You're smarter than I gave you credit for," Wells lamented. "But whatever I did, you can't get me for Jim's murder because he isn't dead!"

I squinted towards the captain, "Is that enough of a confession for you?"

He nodded.

I turned to the audience as they whispered among themselves. "I'm sorry for the ruse everyone but, unfortunately, Big Jim James was not recovered. Kimber, would you come out here please?"

The shadow behind the back curtain moved towards the stage and Kimber emerged, dressed in a well-padded chef's outfit. The audience gasped once more. She took a bow with the sweep of her chef's hat for good measure.

Wells shrieked at me, "You hack! You can't do this to me!" He resumed pulling against Miss deDay's hold.

Ship's security came onto the stage and Roo deDay released Wells into their tender care.

Chapter *Fin*

I woke up early to watch from our balcony as we docked in Southampton. The complimentary bathrobe I wore was not complementary to my looks, but it had been mine to use for the duration of the cruise. Which was now over.

I was relieved, but also a bit sad. It hadn't gone anything like I'd planned. I did not pad my resume with a TV appearance as a judge. And I did not get the quality time with my mother I had wanted, but I still thought our relationship was for the better after all that had happened.

My mother and I ate our final breakfast onboard and were then unceremoniously kicked out of what had been our week-long home—the crew had to ready the ship for its next set of passengers. They would start boarding in a few hours and then the Queen Alex 2 would be off on her next sailing. I hoped it wouldn't be as eventful as ours had been.

We walked down the gangplank and into England.

"Are you glad to be back on dry land, Mom?"

"I'm usually happy wherever I am, son. But I'm especially pleased to have gotten to spend this time with you. Thank you for inviting me."

I knew that she was proud of me and didn't think of me as a little boy. I was starting to not feel that way when I was around her, too.

Kimber approached and my mother asked, "Would you two like a moment alone?"

She replied, "That's not necessary, Gloria. I'll say my goodbyes and my little Murphy and I will go off in search of our next adventure." Her pup popped his head up out of her large purse at the mention of his name.

I gave him a scratch behind the ears. "Thank you for your help last night, Kimber, and... well, all of it." Words did not come as easily as they had at our dinner two nights previous.

"Where are you headed next?" my mother asked her.

"I'm going to tour around the UK for a while. I've rented a small cottage in the Cotswold to use as home base. You're welcome to come visit me." She was looking at me but quickly flashed to my mother and added, "I mean both of you."

My mother embraced her. I leaned in and joined an awkward goodbye hug, careful not to squish Kimber's constant companion.

The hound came our way, stack of collected autographs safely in tow and ballcap pulled down tightly with a five o'clock shadow at 9 in the morning.

I smiled at her. "I hope you have a safe trip, Chase."

"Thank you, Mr. Murphy. My sibling is already on the plane from New York. Kimber offered to wait with me at the airport."

"That's very nice of you, Kimber," I said. "I've been meaning to ask, is your producer friend, Monica, going to be okay? She had so much invested in Chefs at Sea."

"She's over the moon! The network reviewed the footage and will be using it for a new reality crime show called Chefs at Odds. They loved Roo deDay and will be shooting additional material, with Cole as the series host."

"That's so amazing for the three of them." I couldn't contain my excitement. "I'll be getting my TV debut after all."

"Oh, sorry Murph. Monica told me they're recasting your part."

Nuts.

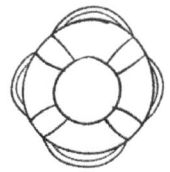

Murph's Pesto Omelet

This deconstructed-pesto-inspired omelet is suitable for brunch, breakfast, or anytime.

> 2 teaspoons olive oil
> 1 clove garlic
> 3 eggs
> salt
> 2 slices provolone cheese
> fresh basil leaves
> 1 tablespoon pine nuts (optional)
> English muffin
> butter
> Golden Shred (orange marmalade)

If using the optional pine nuts, toast them in a dry pan over medium heat for a couple of minutes and set them aside.

Add a couple of teaspoons of olive oil and a minced clove of garlic to a medium-heated pan.

Whisk the eggs in a small bowl and add a few shakes of salt, to taste. Add the eggs to the pan and let them cook until it is almost set.

Turn off the heat then layer the provolone cheese onto half the omelet and cover the pan with a lid to melt the cheese.

Chiffonade (cut into thin strips) the fresh basil leaves and scatter them on the melted cheese, along with the toasted pine nuts. Fold over the omelet and slide it onto a plate.

Serve with a buttered, toasted English muffin and Golden Shred.

Thank you for reading *Tossed: A Snack-Sized Mystery Cruise*. If you enjoyed it please leave a review on Amazon and/or Goodreads, and tell your friends.

Join Murph on his culinary adventures:
Smoked: A Snack-Sized Mystery
Cracked: A Snack-Sized Mystery
Tossed: A Snack-Sized Mystery Cruise

More at JmarsInk.com.

About the Author

Jeff Schmoyer, a recovering tech entrepreneur, tries to find humor in the everyday world around him. He's had several of his short plays produced and a flash fiction story published in the Pikes Peak Writers anthology, *Journeys into Possibility*. He enjoys a tasty meal and a lively game of cards. Find his books at JmarsInk.com.

Made in the USA
Coppell, TX
29 March 2024